TO THE WARS

By the same author:

The Battle of El Alamein and Beyond,
The Book Guild, 1993

TO THE WARS

G.A. Morris

The Book Guild Ltd
Sussex, England

This book is a work of fiction. The characters and situations in this story are imaginary. No resemblance is intended between these characters and any real persons, either living or dead.

This book is sold subject to the condition that it shall not, by way of trade or otherwise, be lent, re-sold, hired out, photocopied or held in any retrieval system or otherwise circulated without the publisher's prior consent in any form of binding or cover other than that in which this is published and without a similar condition including this condition being imposed on the subsequent purchaser.

The Book Guild Ltd
25 High Street,
Lewes, Sussex

First published 1997
© G.A. Morris 1997
Set in Baskerville

Typesetting by Wordset
Hassocks, West Sussex

Printed in Great Britain by
Antony Rowe Ltd,
Chippenham, Wiltshire

A catalogue record for this book is
available from the British Library

ISBN 1 85776 225 8

Dedicated to the survivors

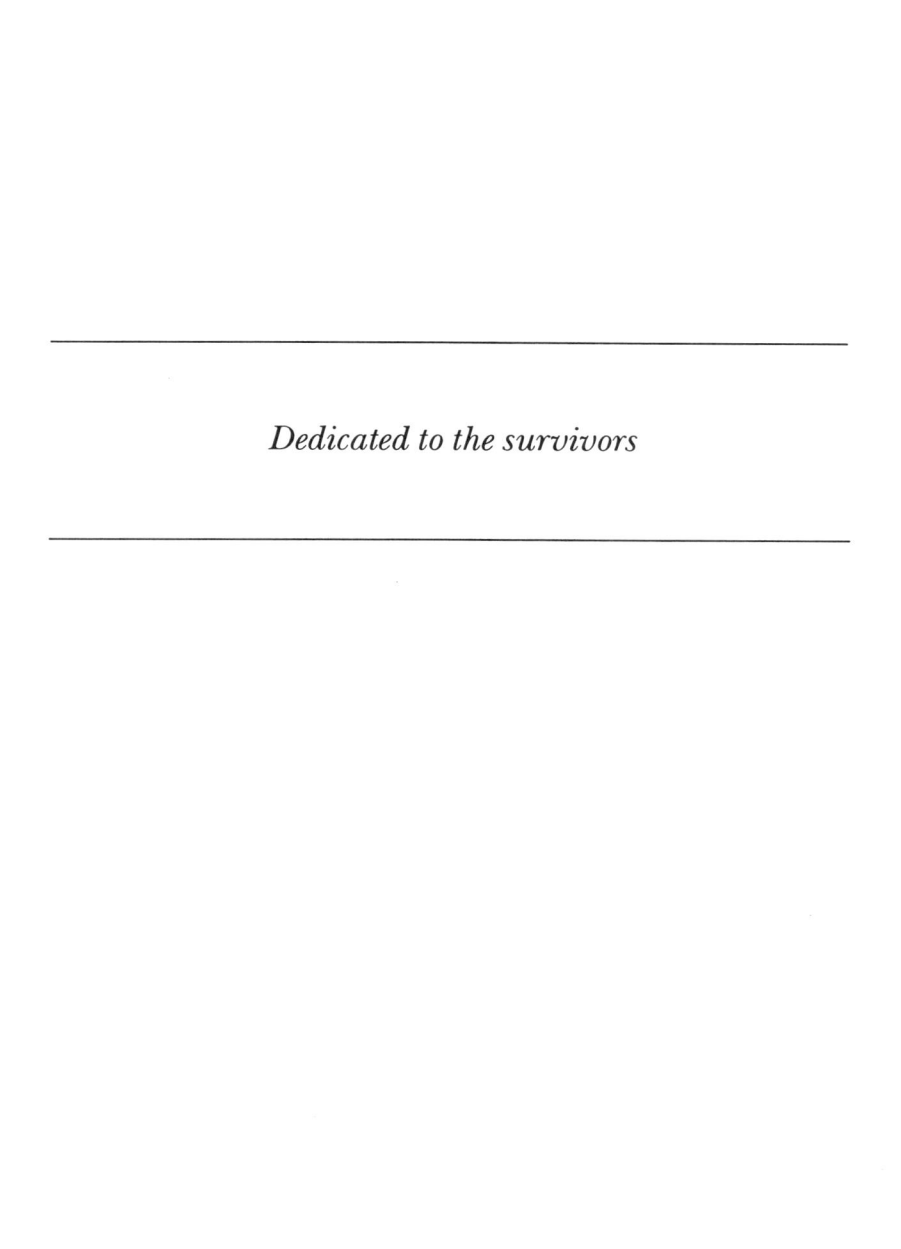

CONTENTS

List of Maps	viii
Principal Characters	ix
The Farm	x
PART ONE – England and the Peninsular War 1808 – 1812	1
PART TWO – America 1812 –1851	49
PART THREE – England and the Crimea 1851 – 1856	81
PART FOUR – America 1857 – 1862	105
PART FIVE – England 1862	113
PART SIX – America 1863 – 1864	123
PART SEVEN – England and France 1865 – 1871	137
PART EIGHT – America, Canada and Cuba 1872 – 1917	145
PART NINE – England and France 1917 – 1918	161
EPILOGUE	175

LIST OF MAPS

The Peninsula	2
The Crimea	88
Balaclava	95
America	106
Gettysburg	130
Belleau and Vierzy	166

PRINCIPAL CHARACTERS

In England

William Collins	– gentleman farmer
James	– his eldest son and heir
John	– younger son, killed in the Peninsular War
William	– James's son, inherited farm

In America

Teresa Collins	– neé Consuela. John Collins's widow
Juan Collins	– son of John and Teresa
Johnny Collins	– son of Juan
James	– son of Johnny
James	– son of James

THE FARM

Collins Farm, North End Village, Hampstead, my maternal ancestors' home for several centuries. Originally, from 1315, it was Wylies Farm.

Part One
England and The Peninsular War
1808–1812

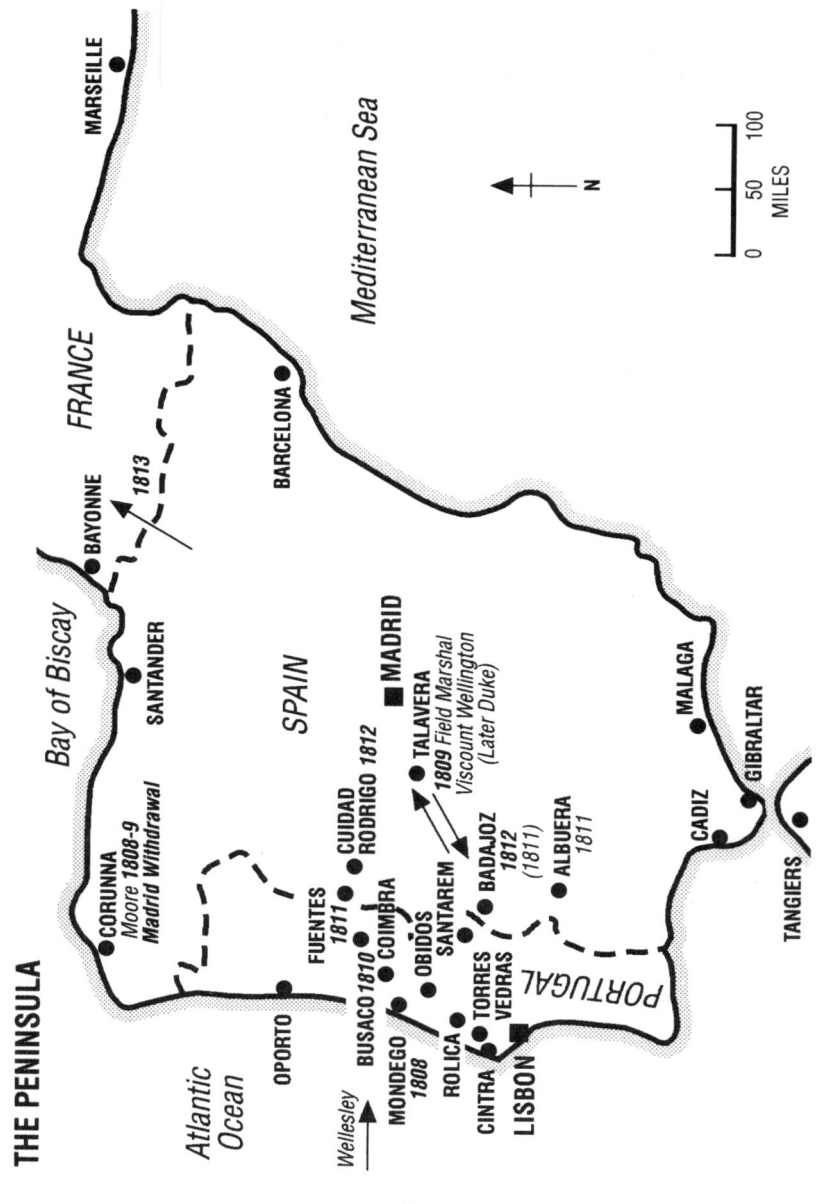

1

John Collins strode purposefully along the track away from the farm where he was born and had lived for all of his twenty years. Pausing to take a last farewell, he set off on his way to adventure. The year was 1808, and Napoleon Bonaparte was rampant on the continent of Europe, seeking world domination. John, the second son of a large family, had no regrets leaving his parents, from whom he had taken a fond farewell the previous evening, and with their blessing and good wishes was off to join the British army, then gathering in a fresh onslaught against the French tyrant.

The Collinses, gentlemen farmers, had worked the farm since the turn of the sixteenth century, modestly successful, their eighty acres of fertile land well-kept and profitable from mixed farming. The origins of the farm dated back to the early fourteenth century when King Edward the Second, the first Prince of Wales, granted manorial rights to the Wylie family and until the Collins family took it over it was known as Wyles Farm, in the parish of Hampstead on the northern outskirts of London. The rents from this farm and others in the neighbourhood were given to Eton College by Henry VI, and to the leper colony of St James, of which Eton College was the custodian. In later years it was visited by the painter William Collins, a relative. Wilkie Collins, the novelist, was a frequent guest. The artist John Linnell stayed frequently with his friend, William Blake, and Charles Dickens lodged often, enjoying the peace, quiet and clean country air so beneficial to his writing. Of its later history, more anon.

John paused at the entrance to adjacent Wildwood Farm to wait for his sweetheart, Doris Cooke, daughter of the farmer. Some two years his junior, very beautiful, auburn-haired and green-eyed, and with a nubile figure, she was much sought after by the boys, but was lovingly attached to the equally attractive young neighbour. John, of average height, sturdily built, very much alive and active, inheriting his good looks from his beautiful mother, Alice, was suited to Doris's beauty and lovingly amorous temperament. So they made their way across the sandy heath, east of the North End Road, for a farewell tryst.

It was a lovely, sunny morning in the early spring, the gorse bushes aflame with yellow blossom, the close turf spongy and inviting in the den they frequented for their lovemaking. John spread his jacket and they lay closely together, exchanging kisses and he, ever the gentleman, observed the etiquette, fondling her breasts, before she guided his hand between her legs, as customary when they met drawerless. Her uncovered loins gave off a delicious sexual aroma, a most pleasing scent arousing John's already inflamed penis even more, so without delay he thrust into Doris's succulent orifice which was mysteriously opened like a funnel, a feat few women can achieve.

John's furious onslaught caused him to discharge whereupon Doris whispered, 'Darling, don't stop. I want to come,' so he pressed on and when she said, 'It is all right now,' it was too late. John continued thrusting away finally achieving a perfect coupling.

Doris exclaimed, 'Sweetheart, that has probably done the job. It is good that I am betrothed to my father's choice but I shall always treasure your child.'

At Wildwood they said their fond farewell, not in sorrow but with the knowledge that their happy times together would always remain as unforgettable memories.

The young man passed on into North End Village, passing the Hare and Hounds, which he did not frequent, preferring the ales at the Bull and Bush. Both inns dated from the mid-eighteenth century when the Bull was a country house owned by William Hogarth, the painter, converted upon his death to the inn, where he had laid out very attractive gardens. John called for his pot of ale and was was greeted cheerfully by the landlord and the few villagers drinking early on, with whom he was well-known and popular. Collecting his bundle of clothing and small possessions, left with the landlord, he bid goodbye and crossed the Sandy Heath to the Spaniards Inn, another of his favourite watering places. The Spaniards Inn dated back to King James I's reign at the beginning of the seventeenth century. Once the Spanish ambassador lodged there and Dick Turpin is alleged to have used the inn and legend tells of his daring escape from the Bow Street Runners. From saying farewell to the Spaniards he passed along the mile long road to Jack Straw's Castle, completing the triangle of inns. Jack Straw's Castle at the top of the hill, by the Whitestone Pond, owed its origin to the assembly of the adherents of the Peasants' Revolt in 1391, of whom he was the leader. In the bar John encountered one of his father's carters on his way to Covent Garden Market, the horses cooling off from the up-hill slog from North End in the Whitestone pond used often so, for whatever road one took across Hampstead a steep climb was involved. The pond was also good for skating on in the winter and dabbling in in the summer. John requested a lift. The cart passed down Haverstock Hill, through Camden and at Charing Cross John got down with the carter's good wishes for the young man's declared intention to join the colours.

From Charing Cross John made his way on foot to the Duke of York's Headquarters at King's Road, Chelsea. The Duke of York was then commander-in-chief of the army.

The sergeant of the guard said, 'Well young man, just go to the orderly room and you are in.'

Having received the King's shilling and been sworn in, John committed, whatever, to be a soldier, requested to join a cavalry regiment. The officer, a cavalry man himself, approved and said that he would send him with a draft to Knightsbridge that same day. The half dozen men walked to the barracks in Knightsbridge in charge of a sergeant. Thereafter, no more walking, only marching with arms swinging. Cavalry men march surprisingly well with a heel to toe movement which jangles the spurs, with a smart kind of pride. At the barracks they were taken over by an old corporal, fed a meagre meal and kitted out with canvas coveralls and forage caps and their civilian clothes were taken away. Any other small possessions could be kept in a knapsack, money and valuables on the person.

'So,' the corporal told them, 'tonight you are free. Tomorrow, at dawn, you leave for the regiment, with remounts and stores' wagon. Those untrained to ride can travel on the wagon. Be back before midnight. John walked down to Hyde Park Corner into Piccadilly, trying to look soldier-like, not unsuccessfully as he had a naturally upright, well-proportioned body. He went into the public bar of The Coach and Horses for a few jars of ale, intending to return in good time for the morrow's long journey. On the way out he was accosted by a pretty young whore and decided to go with her. She was lissom, very young, bright and attractive, so off they went to her dingy room at the back of Shepherd's Market. She held out her hand and he gave her his King's shilling.

'If not enough I have more. That is my joining for a soldier money.'

'It is sufficient,' she said. 'You are much nicer than the men who usually come here. My name is Rosy. What's yours?'

'I am John, off to the the wars. My father is a farmer and, growing tired of the life, I am away for some excitement'

Rosy, stripping off her clothes, caused John to rise up and he lay on the bed waiting for her. Rosy climbed on top, sitting astride saying that she liked it that way and also was safe, having that week been ridded of a child by an old woman's knitting needle.

After some gentle humping Rosy said, 'It hurts too much but I will do something nice for you,' and took him into her mouth, when he soon had an orgasm.

They walked back to the Coach where John bought brandy for himself and port for Rosy, thanking her for a pleasant departure to a new life, drank up and went happily back to barracks and a straw-filled palliasse on the floor, thinking of the morrow and the ride to Shorncliffe Camp, a day's journey into Kent.

2

At Shorncliffe, facing Napoleon across The Channel, was the Rifle Corps with distinctive green uniforms and dark accoutrements, armed with the Baker rifle, a high-precision weapon compared with the smooth bore musket of the line infantry. Attached to the three regiments of rifles was the 14th Hussars, Light Cavalry, whose role was for reconnaissance raids and to protect the Rifles from flank attacks by the French when engaged. General Sir John Moore was responsible for training this experimental group, departing from the orthodox harsh discipline and aiming at an amalgam of team work and individual initiative, a new contribution to the art of warfare. Sir John, the thinking fighting man encouraged by officers who shared the discipline of team work and comradeship, enabled the Light Brigade to become an example to the rest of the British army. The Hussars consisted of a headquarters squadron with a lieutenant colonel and three fighting squadrons, one specially trained for reconnaissance, an independent command hitherto unknown in the army.

John's draft was diverted to the stores in charge of a corporal to be fitted out with uniforms, including the cavalrymen's dolman, a cloak hanging from the left shoulder, altogether very splendid. Weapons were very comprehensive; sword and carbine supplemented by a pair of pistols. Finally the group was allocated to a troop, one of the five of a fighting squadron, received by the troop sergeant, a formidably experienced soldier, and later the troop officer, a very gorgeous young man, foppish in appearance but with an underlying strength and intelligence.

There followed weeks of training in the art of employing their assortment of weapons, troop exercises and, above all, the combination of fire and movement. In their spare time off duty they were allowed out into the surrounding countryside, not made too welcome by the locals and avoided by the women and girls who sensed that any trafficking would be unprosperous. Nevertheless, it was a very pleasant time in the fruitful summer weather.

So in July 1808 they embarked in transports and set sail for Spain under the command of General Sir Arthur Wellesley, later to be Field Marshall Duke of Wellington. The men in the crowded transports were in high spirits, an armada of some nine thousand soldiers, going on a crusade to defeat the wily French then rampaging through Spain. Wellesley went ahead to Corunna where he found conflicting information regarding the state of the Spanish forces and the enemy. After consultation with the commanding admiral he decided to land at Mondego Bay, south of Oporto in Portugal, and from there to march to Lisbon, some eighty miles away, the base for further operations.

The coast was exposed to Atlantic rollers and tumultuous surf, inhospitable, but, most importantly, the landing was unopposed. John's transport to the north of the fleet disembarked into flat-bottomed boats, he with a pair of horses with rope halters, and were towed to the shore by sailors into the huge breakers: indescribable turmoil. The horses were justifiably alarmed and struggled frantically, plunging into the surf and dragging poor John, who clung fast to the halters, into a mêlée of flying hooves. He received a fearsome glancing blow to the head and chest, became almost unconscious and collapsed on the sandy shore, to pass out stranded like a landed fish.

He regained his senses aware that he was in a bed, and looking down at him was a strange but beautiful face, that of a young woman.

She said, 'Do not move. You are somewhat injured, your head and ribs. We found you on a lonely part of the shore.'

The young woman explained that she was Teresa Consuelo, widow of a Spanish exporter of wines to England, where she had often stayed on her husband's visits and had learnt to speak English. Her husband had recently been robbed and killed by bandits and she was living in her mother's house at a village outside Coimbra, some few kilometres from Mondego. John became aware that his head was bandaged and his chest strapped tightly, a confliction of aches and pains. Teresa fetched her mother, Pilar Zinho, a striking elderly version of her daughter, and together they bathed poor John, fed him and left him to rest.

After a few days it was obvious that a mutual attraction had grown between Teresa and John. John was aroused and Teresa, long without a man, was all too compliant, managing in spite of his immobility to successfully mount upon her with little discomfort and much pleasure.

So John, young and healthy, well and lovingly cared for, quickly recovered and after about three weeks he informed Teresa and her mother, Pilar, 'My love, I am now well and must rejoin my regiment but I cannot bear to leave you. Why must we part? It is too cruel.'

Teresa, of the same mind, proposed, 'John, I am free and with my mother's blessing I am ready to go wherever you wish.'

Pilar agreed, saying, 'Yes, I see that you really love each other. Why not get married now and go with clear consciences?'

The village priest was willing and John did not disclose that he was not of the Catholic faith. The wedding was well-attended. Teresa's family was very popular and, being more fortunate than most, were generous to their less well-endowed neighbours.

It was decided that Teresa and John would purchase a small wagon drawn by two horses for Teresa and a charger for John. Both of them were well-endowed, he with the money concealed in his clothing, which was intact, and she with the considerable wealth left her by her husband, Juan.

They departed en route to rejoin Wellesley's army on a hot summer morning, south to Lisbon, the cart well-stocked and John's horse tethered behind, both full of a sense of well-being and happy to be together.

The road showed signs of the passing of the army; discarded bits and pieces, litter of all kinds. John was able to replenish the lost and worn parts of his uniform and equipment and, apart from the scar on his head, had nothing to show for his unfortunate mishap. He was once more the smart, young trooper.

Then followed a journey of some hundred miles through a countryside of gardens of aloes and cypresses, vineyards and olive groves, undulating hills, wooded heights and barren valleys, the occasional bullock carts screeching along on solid wheels, the drivers striding along handy with their tormenting goads. Camping by night in secluded groves, with a cheerful camp fire, the air filled with the scents of sage and rosemary, with a background voice of frogs and cicadas, John and Teresa were at blissful ease. They gave little thought to the coming days and the uncertainty of the future.

The French, aware of the advance on Lisbon by Wellesley, had crossed the River Tagus and were advancing along the Lisbon-Mondego road, where scouts from the British encountered them at Obidos where the French had taken up a strong position. John and Teresa encountered the straggle of the camp followers and the commissariat wagons and, leaving Teresa with the cart among the numerous wives and ladies, John rode on to the front where could be heard desultory musket fire. Encountering fighting troops, he politely requested an officer to direct him to the 14th Hussars, which he was rejoining. The regiment was a few miles along the road to the right flank of the British and Portuguese force flanking Obidos. John located his troop and the officer, so pleased to see him, long thought to be lost in the landing, explained that he was just in time for the attack on the French in Obidos, where the Hussars were ordered to destroy a troublesome battery flanking the approach to the town.

The Hussars walked the horses along a dry river bed, fanning out at the trot to the open ground still concealed from the French and the objective: two squadrons up with one in reserve, John's troop on the extreme right flank. As the guns came into sight the squadrons, still unobserved, broke into a canter and then, when dozy pickets raised the alarm, firing their muskets ineffectively at the advancing horsemen, the cavalry galloped full tilt at the battery. Frantic efforts to turn the guns were too late and the Hussars were in among them cutting down the gunners who attempted resistance. John bloodied his sword by running through a pistol-firing artillery officer. Throughout the excitement of the charge, their first action, there was only exhilaration and very few casualties; three hit by random fire from the battery guard section. A trooper galloped off to let the main body know that the battery was taken out.

The light infantry divisions advanced and after a bloody skirmish dashed after the retreating French until halted by intensive fire from the main body outside Rolica, losing several officers and riflemen. The army consolidated on the plain before Rolica, the men lolling on the grass eating their rations of beef and hardtack biscuits, drinking hoarded grog or Portuguese wine from their canteens.

Meanwhile, a squadron of the 14th carried out a reconnaissance patrol close to the French lines, too near perhaps because a burst of musketry felled some of the troopers, including the troop sergeant of John's troop; a first rather sobering blooding.

At dawn the main body moved on Rolica with two regiments in advance, storming a defile on the Lisbon road. Despite heavy losses the two regiments pressed on, holding the French until Wellesley let go the rest and by the end of the day several hundred prisoners were taken and many guns. The road to Torres Vedras was open and Wellesley knew that the important battle to advance against Lisbon, the first against the might of the Imperial Legions,

Napoleon's pride, was to begin. The object was to secure Lisbon, the only suitable harbour where the fleet could shelter from the Atlantic gales and provide a base for further Peninsula operations. The Hussars, meanwhile, had been scouting along a coastal track to probe a route round Torres Vedras.

'Collins,' said the troop officer, 'Leave your weapons here except for pistols and proceed on foot as close as possible to the French lines outside Torres Vedras (which was just in view over the ridge in front). Report back on anything that you observe.'

With some trepidation John went off in the early dusk, all around eerie and foreboding shadows lurking in concealment.

After a mile or so there was no sign of movement when suddenly from both sides he heard, '*Halt, qui va la?*' and covered by two French soldiers, muskets levelled at him, he had no chance to run. '*Ah, un soldat Anglais. Venez, vite.*' So John was escorted to the nearest guard post on the outskirts of the town and locked up in a bare cell with an iron-barred window near the ceiling and left miserable and hungry to await whatever the morning brought. At dawn he was roughly wakened, given some dry bread, cheese and poor coffee, and then taken before an officer who said, 'I know who you are from, the cavalry who destroyed our battery at Obidos.' Being their first British soldier prisoner, he was a great curiosity and as such paraded through the busy streets, attracting the attention of one particular onlooker, of whom more later.

That night he was awakened in his cell by pebbles thrown from the window and as he roused a voice said, 'Soldier, I am Major Charles Murray, an exploring officer. You will be released before dawn by partisans and brought to me.'

Some while later there was a scuffle outside the cell door, which was quickly opened, and he was hustled out through the guard room where lay four dead guards, by raggedly dressed but dangerously armed Portuguese partisans.

Moving rapidly through back streets, they entered a house where Major Murray waited, a very undistinguished-looking man, disguised in the clothes of a prosperous shopkeeper, part of his cover as a spy, an intelligence agent.

'I have a very urgent despatch for Sir Arthur Wellesley,' he said. 'You are heaven-sent. These men will take you through the enemy lines. Report to your officer. A note is enclosed for his attention. Good luck. Perhaps we shall meet again.'

Using unfrequented paths, the partisans arrived at a position away from the French and indicated the direction that he should take to find his unit. John's officer was relieved to see him, thinking him lost, and astonished at the extraordinary story of his capture and escape. The letter intended for himself informed him that as the bearer knew his identity it might prove advantageous to use Collins as a courier at some future date and to deliver the despatch to the general immediately.

On his return, having consulted with the squadron commander, he informed John that he would be promoted acting sergeant and that he might one day be required to contact Major Murray.

The army had now taken up position outside Torres Vedras, which put the 14th Hussars on the right flank toward the sea. The French, forestalling the British, levelled a further attack aimed at destroying them entirely. The army fought back ferociously and before the day's end had the French on the run towards Lisbon. The Hussars were advanced forward to get into Cintra on the coast outside Lisbon. The cavalry set out on a fine sunny day. The countryside, although dry, was pleasantly wooded, and they went jogging down the coastal tracks, bent on the cavalry's prime tasks of reconnaissance and marauding. Most of the twenty-five miles were covered without incident, John's squadron leading with the troop scouting ahead. Approaching a wood near Cintra, they surprised a small group of French infantry busily eating their midday meal. Too late to stop them, several fired at the troop, who quickly overcame them, but too late; the alarm was evident in the movement of the forces on the outskirts of Cintra, which was estimated to be only a small force. The troop fell back to the main body of the cavalry and upon the receipt of the situation report the colonel decided to attack, abandoning the role of reconnaissance. The squadron moved out into line abreast, advancing with gathering momentum encountering the first of the defenders at the charge, an awesome sight to the French, who initially crumbled, but resistance increased with steady musketry from the outskirts of the town. The troopers were soon in among the enemy , slashing and thrusting with their swords. The apparently second-rate infantry fled with the troopers firing their carbines and pistols effectively. There were few casualties to the Hussars and most of the French were rounded up and taken prisoner. It was a very successful event. Cintra became an important base for Wellesley, who established his headquarters there. The army established itself outside Lisbon on the River Tagus, joined by reinforcements from England so forming the whole of the British forces in the Peninsula, poised to strike out of Portugal into Spain.

The army settled down to winter in Portugal. The commissariat and camp followers joined up and there were joyful reunions and commiserations for the several new widows who could choose to stay on or chance a passage on a homeward-bound ship. It was better perhaps, to remain and find another protector among the many who were available and willing.

Teresa was overjoyed to be reunited with John, ensconced in the snug van which sometimes rocked from their strenuous lovemaking. Teresa was enthralled by John's adventures and promotion. She, due to her obvious good breeding and position, had become the queen bee of the regimental ladies, well-liked by all.

The winter passed in much training and accommodating the new recruits and old soldiers from the now extinct northern army in Spain. Wellesley adhered to the principle of intensive training established by the now late Sir John Moore, who had brought the Rifle Corps of Green Jackets to the forefront of light infantry. Their performance in the initial campaign had proved the success of Sir John's hard training and emphasized the importance of military preparation so that the army in the Peninsula was effectively one of the best ever to take to the field.

Sir John Moore had been in command of the army in the north which landed at Corunna. He had achieved an incredible success, a series of battles which took them into Madrid. Napoleon was enraged and ordered his marshals at all costs to relieve Madrid. Let down by his Spanish allies, Sir John Moore was forced into retreat, ending up with the withdrawal from Corunna by means of a vast fleet of transports, marshalled by the Royal Navy. Most of those experienced troops ended up with Wellesley. Sir John Moore was killed by enemy fire during the evacuation, a tragic loss.

3

In the Spring of 1809 Wellesley was planning to advance to Talavera where the French were massed. Fortuitously, Major Murray was in the town and passed a message to the commander-in-chief that he required a courier. The colonel of the 14th being informed sent for John and the squadron and troop officer. The colonel informed them that Sgt Collins was to proceed with a guide to Santarem, some hundred miles east towards the frontier with Spain, and seek out Major Murray at a location known to the guide. The sergeant would be in uniform; otherwise if caught, he would be shot out of hand. The troop officer rapidly considered the use of Teresa and told the colonel that it would be advantageous to send John with his Portuguese wife, who, formerly married to a Spanish merchant, spoke the language and knew the country well, having travelled widely with the late husband. They also had their own cart. This was agreed and they returned to the squadron lines to inform Teresa and make the necessary arrangements.

Teresa was delighted to stay with John, who, under the circumstances, would be travelling in civilian clothes and carrying only his pistols, as a sick man, very ill with contagious fever, going back to Santarem to her family. Well-provisioned and with extra warm clothing, it would be very cold in the Sierras although late spring, they set off with John's horse on a lead behind the cart.

For two days they travelled by unfrequented roads but, obliged to travel a short distance along the Madrid main road, ran into a French patrol of dragoons whose officer, upon learning of the case of disease, gave them a *laissez-passer* and hurried them on, not bothering to look closely at

John who quickly got under the blankets inside the cart.

In another five days they reached Santarem which appeared to be only lightly held by the French; no outposts or defensive works, obviously not intended to be contested should Wellesley dare to move out against the very superior army. Teresa enquired the whereabouts of the house where the occupants informed John that the English officer had gone, leaving a message for the courier. The note informed John to proceed on well inside Spain on the way to Madrid, another kettle of fish to travel so far in enemy held territory. With caution and not a little anxiety they crossed the border into Spain, encountering a few outposts and patrols without hindrance since there were many such travellers on the more frequented roads.

At dusk one evening, passing into the Sierra foothills through a grove of pines, they were baulked by two villainous looking men. One was musket-armed, the other brandishing a dangerous looking knife. John rapidly drew his pistols from handy concealment and shot the armed robber through the head, he immediately became a very dead bandit. The other fled and, after dragging the corpse into the undergrowth, Teresa and John continued onwards. After some days, uneventfully passing through some small villages, they approached their goal, Talavera, when it was thought best to leave John with the cart and for Teresa to locate the major, riding the horse which was delighted when untied from the cart.

Teresa found the house and identified herself to Major Murray who was delighted to meet such a beautiful messenger and, having wined and supped Teresa, sent her off for John, pleased that they had reached him safely.

The major greeted John warmly, congratulated him on his lovely and courageous wife and was very pleased when he was told that his courier was promoted to sergeant.

'Stay the night and rest well,' he said, 'you must depart at dawn and make your way back as rapidly as possible but with precaution not to be taken. The contents of my despatch are of the utmost importance and must be destroyed if there is a real danger of them falling into French hands. You must deliver to the general in person and I will provide you with a letter to that effect, to enable you to pass without let or hindrance once you reach our controlled area in Portugal.'

So at crack of dawn they were on the road, their cover story being that of a Portuguese wife taking her incurably sick Spanish husband, stricken down by an awful disease, to her home in Coimbra to stay with her mother. The return journey was uneventful. When halted by the rare military post their cover was accepted and the soldiers even avoided looking at John. Once into Portugal they made all haste into the English controlled area and John took to his horse and with the special letter speeded on to the general, introducing himself as the courier from Major Murray at Talavera bearing urgent despatches, Sergeant Collins of the 14th Hussars. Wellesley was well-pleased, and over a map extracted from John details of his journey and whatever information he could about the countryside, all being carefully noted by a staff officer.

The General dismissed John saying, 'I am well pleased with your efforts. You will be rewarded and I will now give you a letter for your colonel. It is very likely that we shall meet again.'

On John's return to the regiment he reported to the colonel, having first changed into uniform, accompanied by the squadron officer.

The colonel, after reading the letter from Sir Arthur which John handed to him, said, 'The general is pleased with you, having brought the information vital to the forthcoming operations, together with your own useful observations of the countryside. Please convey my thanks to your wife for her role in this mission.'

After John left the colonel said to the two officers that he would like information as to the sergeant's background and told them to watch his behaviour during the future operations.

'He may well be worth considering for a move out of the ranks,' he said. 'I know that that is unusual but what he has done has been carried out on the field of battle.'

Teresa and her equipage returned the following day and they settled into a blissful period in camp: soldier husband and regimental wife.

In July 1809 Wellesley proposed an advance towards Talavera with the not inconsiderable Spanish army in Portugal with the two Light Infantry Brigades and the Hussars in support, under the command of the Spanish general. Not only the Spanish army moved forward. They brought along with them an impossible entourage of commissariat, wives, carts, wagons and even live animals. The riflemen were astonished and the British contingent tagged along behind the motley assembly of gorgeous attired military and the ragged uncontrollable followers. Of course, the inevitable happened some thirty miles on, they ran into the bulk of a French corps of some fifty thousand men and fled in utter confusion back down the Madrid road, passing through the Light Division which rapidly deployed into a defensive line with the Hussars on either flank. The British fought a stubborn rearguard action, the cavalry harassing the following French troops who, fortunately, were slack to seize the opportunity due to uncertainty of advancing into a hostile, barren country.

Wellesley then took command, rallied the Spanish forces and, with tremendous drive, forced a way through the high ground outside Talavera, with the Spanish in a reserve position from the Tagus river to the right of the town, the British drawn up facing the massed French divisions firmly established along a small stream, a tributary of the Tagus. The night passed uncomfortably, especially for the British, far from their base and very short of supplies, the troops on half-rations. Wellesley ordered an attack at dawn led by the Light Division and the Hussars who were in the centre of the opposing French.

At first light the cavalry advanced, line abreast with the front rank light infantry clinging to the stirrups. Desultory artillery fire broke out, not very effective, too few guns being available. The division reached the stream, still out of musket range, but shortly were under fierce fire from the French division to their front. The officers out in front broke into a canter and the infantry were obliged to let go of the stirrups and to follow at their fastest pace, speedier than other infantry. The Hussars, now at the gallop, were under close and accurate musket fire. Many fell, including John's troop officer, so he rode to the front of the troop in the officer's leading place. The shock of the charge and the ensuing mêlée dented the formation and the infantry fought their way into the French, causing the immediate troops to fall back. Meanwhile, the army, including the Spanish, closely behind the Light Division, engaged the whole of the massed French at close quarters. The French, in superior numbers and all seasoned troops, held and the Spaniards, never very brave, retreated in disorder. Wellesley had no option but to pull back to the former positions, fairly secure on the high ground. The French consolidated their force across the stream, closer to the British.

The division and the Hussars had suffered many casualties, mostly dead, few wounded got back, and spent the night regrouping, eating their meagre rations and sleeping as well as possible. John was to take over the troop temporarily and, although slightly wounded in the leg by a French bayonet, he managed. During the night the French launched exploratory attacks against the British. There was then a preliminary cavalry attack against the weak spot of the line, the Spanish, who discharged their muskets ineffectively and the whole Spanish line instantaneously fled.

It was forced then upon the British to pull back or be surrounded and lost. Wellesley realized that there was no alternative but to withdraw from Spain; there was no line to be held before Portugal and the previous base. With the Light Infantry and the Hussars, now the most experienced division in the field (generals do have favourite units who in consequence are hardworked. 'Why is it always us?') covering the rearguard, they went in a reasonably orderly way back through inhospitable country, generally keeping ahead of the oncoming French, and the army regained its former positions, back where it began.

The French reoccupied most of Portugal, Santarem, Obidos, Rolica and were halted outside Torres Vedras, which was also taken. The French were now overstretched too far from their supply base and the hostile territory had little to offer. Wellesley was secure, adequately supplied from England by a splendid fleet of supply ships and the invincible Royal Navy, unchallenged after Nelson's victory at Trafalgar in 1805.

It might have been a different story if the Spanish had stood at Talavera but at least Wellesley knew that he could never rely on them as a strong ally.

Wellesley returned to England and was called to account for the rashness of his summer campaign, the casualties of his soldiers, the loss of wounded and the hardships of the retreat from Talavera. However, in spite of his enemies he was elevated to the peerage as Viscount Wellington (later Duke of Wellington and field marshal) and granted a lifetime annual gratuity by Parliament. Lord Wellington returned to Spain as commander-in-chief of the army, now gathering strength, augmented from England and secure from the French.

4

John and Teresa settled down to blissful married life, snug in the cart and the envy of others less well-provided. Teresa was well supplied with her late husband's gold and with plentiful supplies from England they lived all too well.

John's duties required regular attendance with the troop which, failing a replacement officer, he was commanding. There were many additions to the army, fresh troops from England, from illustrious regiments of guards and the cavalry, building up a formidable force preparing for the forthcoming campaigns of 1810, above all, very well-trained and being further honed during the build up winter months. Occasional reconnaissance patrols were sent out to the east and north, making visual contact with the French outposts and sometimes picking up straying soldiers not unhappy to be taken prisoner.

John took his troop one eventful day to probe into a village towards Cintra, ground which they well knew from the previous year. Approaching the area, the troop dismounted and John sent a section forward to get unobserved into the village, which consisted of only a dozen or so dwellings. With the interpreter and with great fortune they contacted a Portuguese farmer going out to the fields. He informed them that there were ten French soldiers under a sergeant, not very active and using the largest house, which he pointed out. The section returned and John decided to approach on foot with the whole troop on foot, carbines at the ready. It was a simple operation. The enemy were all in the house with the exception of one soldier coming from the outside toilet who was too dumbfounded to raise the alarm and quickly taken.Rushing the house from front and back, the surprise was completely successful. The bearded sergeant, an old soldier, fired his pistol at the leading trooper, who was wounded in the arm and the sergeant was promptly shot dead by the following man. The rest were cowed, herded into one room, secured and barred and warned that any noise or disturbance from them and they would be shot. The interpreter told them that he was informed that the relief soldiers were due that evening and John decided to ambush them at the point where the track entered the village, from concealment in and around the houses. Sure enough, in the late afternoon the relief of some dozen infantrymen ambled down the track and when well within range, the troop opened fire, downing four of them, including their sergeant. The others immediately surrendered and joined their comrades in captivity: a good bag.

They were told that a young French woman was being hidden in the village, a runaway French officer's woman, escaping from his brutal ill-treatment of her. He produced the lady after eliciting where she was from her protectors. She was a very beautiful young woman who said that she was Marie Longlon and confirmed that she was indeed running away from the French officer. They set off without delay, Marie riding her own horse. By a woman's instinct she kept close to the gallant, handsome sergeant.

Pushing on as fast as the walking prisoners could be made to go, the company arrived back at camp, to be greeted with astonishment. John reported back to his squadron leader who was full of praise for the very successful operation. He ordered John, the girl Marie, who as a 'deserter' could be expected to tell all she knew of the French, together with the prisoners who would be interrogated, to escort them to headquarters. Word spread through the regiment and John was warmly welcomed by all. Teresa was enthralled but, perhaps a little irritated over Marie, whom John described to her with some unconcealed warmth, Teresa indicated that perhaps Marie could come to her as a companion and servant – a fatal mistake.

After consulting the colonel it was decided to take the unusual step of promoting John to acting lieutenant as the colonel had received additional information on John's background, which confirmed that he came of good yeoman stock, long established in their county and not unsuited to hold the King's Commission. The Yeomanry were, in fact, to become the principal source of officers and other ranks for the cavalry, but, of course, the elite regiments still attracted the aristocracy.

John, overwhelmed, was told that his rank would be confirmed when Lord Wellington returned. Meanwhile, he could take over his own troop, or another if he thought that the other ranks might not accept him as one of them. John said that he preferred the old troop since the men had already willingly accepted him in charge as a sergeant, ex-trooper, so it was. He was able to obtain officer's kit from the commissariat dead officer's wagon at headquarters and would henceforth be quartered in the officers' lines. Teresa would take a small house, retaining the cart for further field operations. She also acquired a smart carriage, not being in the least short of funds. In due course Marie returned and was welcomed by Teresa as a companion, although she was a little concerned by Marie's shy, obvious pleasure in seeing John again, especially now he was a gallant, young officer. So they settled down to a totally different life. Teresa was accepted by the other officers' wives. John met little resentment from the other regimental officers; after all, he was very presentable, smart and every bit a soldier, apart from being well able to defend himself against any physical display of insult. He was also, in a small way, known personally to Lord Wellington due to his activities as a courier on secret missions, a fact inevitably not entirely unknown of by some.

They settled down to a very pleasant period. There was extensive training, the keynote of Wellington's preparations, but John had sufficient time to spend with Teresa in her small house. Marie was unobtrusively around but subconsciously both John and Teresa were aware of the bridled, strong attraction that John had for the younger woman.

In the early days of 1810 Teresa decided that she must travel to see her mother at Coimbra, now well inside the French lines. It was agreed that she should make the journey and travel by fishing boat from Lisbon to Mondego, a somewhat dangerous voyage in the Atlantic seas, turbulent in winter, but with little chance of being caught by the enemy. A willing fisherman was located who knew the run up the coast very well and who would convey Teresa for a fairly tidy sum of gold and arrange to pick her up after a week on shore; little time but sufficient for Teresa's purpose. So off she went, somewhat anxious to leave John with Marie around.

The first time that John went to the house they met and no word was spoken. Marie with savage desire, flung herself at John whose response was equally passionate and without delay they rushed to the bedroom, shedding clothing on the way. Marie was unbelievably desirable, simply made for love, wide open to receive John who was more than ready. Their lovemaking was tremendous, orgasms one after another for a full half day. Neither had experienced such devastating passion, uncaring of the consequences. All too aware of Teresa's imminent return, they crammed in as much sex as possible so that even in such a short time John had lost considerable weight and vigour, an inevitable consequence of too much lovemaking; but naturally, Marie was blooming.

Teresa returned after a month's absence and a successful although hazardous journey, bringing with her those possessions that she was able to ship on the small boat which had returned to Mondego as arranged. But more importantly, she brought the remainder of her wealth.

By misfortune, the delinquent pair of lovers were in the house, not, it happened, in an embarrassing situation but what had gone on was obvious to Teresa. She saw a tattered John and Marie like a contented cat, almost purring. Without hesitation, Teresa ordered Marie to leave immediately and never return on pain of punishment.

'You are an alien, a French citizen, of the enemy,' she said.

'My husband rescued you, I befriended you and this is how you repay us.' Marie did not make a fuss. After all, by her previous situation as a French officer's woman, she was of easy virtue and would very easily make a life for herself in Lisbon. John was chastened but secretly relieved. Teresa loved him and would forgive him but it was always there in the background and upon occasion, when the inevitable marital quarrel arose, Teresa would openly taunt John with Marie's and his relationship and shameful behaviour, weakly denied by John.

In the spring the colonel sent for John and informed him that he was to carry out a mission to contact the exploring Major, who was at Obidos. John would go alone and in uniform, which was safer if he were caught, and he accepted the suggestion that the journey would be made by the sea route to a place on the shore nearest to Obidos, thereby avoiding the perilous passage through Torres Vedras which was heavily guarded by the main army in Spain of the French. The colonel said that the Duke of Wellington was pleased to see John again and congratulated him on his promotion and the incident which led to it being awarded.

The general dismissed his staff, saying to John, 'There is certain information that I require from Major Murray which I have written down. You will commit this to memory and destroy the paper before entering enemy held territory. In addition, you will carry a large sum of money for the major's use.'

John told Teresa that he was going away. He gave no details but said that he wished to contact the fisherman who had conveyed Teresa. Arrangements were concluded. The fishing boat would land John on a sandy beach that they knew of to the west of Obidos, a voyage of some hundred miles, close to the coast; not an unusual journey, just another fishing vessel. Obidos was about forty miles from the coast and John planned to cover this distance by night on the track they had previously used the year before when advancing to Cintra. To remain in uniform and yet be inconspicuous, he chose officers' coveralls used occasionally at stables, a forage cap and a voluminous plain dark cloak. As weapons, he carried his pistols, a carbine and a vicious long Portuguese knife. His few necessities and the money bag were packed in a soldier's knapsack. He also carried a large canteen filled with water weakly mixed with brandy, a magnetic compass and a small pocket telescope.

They set off from Lisbon at dawn, aiming to arrive at the beach before dawn five days hence. They had a good southeast wind, with the boat moving before it at a comfortable speed and motion, a quarter moon providing sufficient light for safe sailing by night and spring weather likely to last. Just before dawn, the sky lightening, they arrived off the beach and John was carried through the shallows by two sailors, to avoid tell-tale wet legs.

The beach was deserted and John rapidly moved inland a few miles out over the coastal track, finding a good hiding place in the cover of a dense copse with a good view over the approaches. The day passed pleasantly. He ate and drank sparsely from his small supplies, observing the ground up to the track. There was very little movement: a few carts and pedestrians on the track, nothing to disturb him. At dusk he moved off across country on a bearing which would take him on the way to Obidos and he would eventually reach territory he was familiar with.

A completely uneventful two nights of walking brought him in sight of the town when he laid up in concealment until dusk, when he moved openly into the outskirts to the main square, meeting a few people hurrying to their homes and supper and so found the house in a side street.

Major Murray was delighted to see him and congratulated the young officer on his well-deserved promotion. John handed over the money and together they worked over Wellington's requests for information, which were added to the despatches that John would be taking back. It seemed that there was little if any military activity in the area, the enemy being concentrated on a line from Badajoz-Santarem-Torres Vedras-Cintra, cutting off the British way into Portugal to the north and Spain to the east.

The rendezvous with the fishing boat was in four days so John set off carefully and without haste to be certain of getting back to Lisbon with the precious despatches which he concealed next to his skin. In addition, now quite an experienced soldier, he was carrying vital information in his head. He arrived safely at the hideout he had used overlooking the coast a day ahead. After nightfall he dozed fitfully, awaiting an hour or so before dawn to get down to the beach. Half asleep, he was rudely awakened by two ruffians obviously intent on robbing him. Before they could overpower him, his two pistols concealed under his cloak were aimed at them and by good fortune one bullet struck the nearest man in the chest. The other hesitated and John was on him with the long knife, thumb on the blade and as he struck up the drill was successfully carried out. The result was two very dead rascals. Because of the noise of the pistol shots, John decided to drag the bodies hastily into concealment and to clear out as near to the beach as was secure. Fortunately, there was no reaction by any who might detect him and just before dawn he spotted the boat. Not needing to be carried through the surf, he rushed into the sea, clambered aboard and was away.

When safely at Lisbon, he went immediately to Wellington, looked at askance by those he had to pass before gaining admission. Although scruffily dressed John was nonetheless an impressive figure, bursting with urgency. Wellington was delighted to see him, received the despatches and listened carefully to John's report.

He said to him, 'Collins, I am very pleased. It is vitally important to receive what you bring. You have done very well and have demonstrated the important achievement of to-see-and-not-be-seen.'

He promised that John would be rewarded in kind, but it was too early for further promotion, although well deserved.

John reported to the colonel after a joyful and albeit

amorous couple of hours. Back in proper uniform, he received his brief unrevealing report and so went back to the squadron where, once more, other than the major, none knew the purpose of his absence. He settled into the troop with pleasure to be back, elated from the success of the mission.

5

The army, now much reinforced, continued training until the summer of 1810 when Wellington decided to thrust northwards against the French forces along the Torres Vedras lines, almost certainly demoralized by the months spent in a hostile territory wasted by the British retreating from Talavera in 1809.

The army moved towards Torres Vedras, the Light Division leading, being superior in firepower and movement, with the 14th Hussars out front, John's squadron ahead in their role of reconnaissance. The Hussars found little sign of enemy movement upon sighting the town, so John was sent in with his troop to take a look. Well, the French had gone, obviously forewarned of the British approach, pulling back to prepared lines further north. The Light Division pushed on at their superior rate, overtaking many stragglers. The French were hard-pressed and unable to halt at Coimbra, so were obliged to cross the Sierras to the east leading to the great plains of Spain, hopefully to join Napoleon's supposedly advancing army in Spain, aware of the British advance.

The Hussars pressed on to Busaco, in the Sierras, and halted on a prominent ridge with sufficient room to deploy the oncoming divisions. The ridge gave clear views toward the sea in the west and the plains to the east where the French movements could be clearly observed. The Light Division straddled the road out of Spain to Coimbra where the French would presumably be expected to attack since it was the only easy way up to the ridge, other approaches being rock-strewn and somewhat difficult for an army to make a consolidated attack. The Hussars were positioned on the flank of the division linking up with the troops adjacent to them.

At dawn next day, from their high positions the British looked down across the plain where as far as the eye could see were long columns glittering in the sunshine, coming along every viable route, steadily approaching from the east, a multitude of foot, horse, guns and teams of wagons. The British, although out-numbered, were not perturbed. Superbly trained and full of confidence, their six divisions faced three French corps. Wellington rode calmly along the front, heightening the confidence of the alert troops. The drums and fifes, a swelling rub-a-dub-dub, grew ever louder as the massed divisions of Marshal Ney's corps advanced, their axis the road in front of the Light Division. The other two French corps were spread out on either flank, seeking tracks and crevices along which to gain the Busaco ridge. The intention of the corps on the right was to cut through at a point where the terrain was easier and to surround the British. In the centre, the French struck against the Light Division where the rifles and shrapnel of the Horse Artillery guns' withering fire slaughtered the oncoming ranks. The Hussars emerged from the flank and hit the French with a furious charge, breaking up the ranks of the nearest division and adding considerably to the rout of Ney's corps which was obliged to withdraw. The other corps were equally repulsed by brisk fire from the British, secure in their ridge top positions.

John's horse, with him since Coimbra, was struck in the foreleg by a musket ball which felled the horse, partially pinning a stunned John under it. Upon recovering, he freed himself and reluctantly shot his horse through the head. It was getting late in the afternoon now. The firing was dying down, so John made his way very cautiously to the Green Jackets in front who, fortunately, recognized the uniform, and so he got back to the regiment.

Wellington knew that he could not possibly hold out for long against the superior numbers of the enemy, but he was well-satisfied that he had demonstrated to Napoleon's men the true mettle of the British fighting man. At nightfall the British pulled out in orderly fashion, barely scratched by the day's encounter, covered by the Light Division and the Hussars, passing through Coimbra after two days of orderly withdrawal.

Unfortunately, the autumnal rains, it being now October, set in with furious downpourings and the withdrawal became more like a retreat, with abandoned wagons bogged down in the mud. A mass of miserable, bedraggled civilians were evacuated for fear of the hated French. The British regiments tramped along soaked by the torrential rain. Gone were the high hopes of the display at Busaco. They were depressed, imagining the future ignominious evacuation from the Peninsula awaiting them. Fortunately for the rearguard, the pursuing French were equally bogged down by the weather and posed little threat. There were no more than a few skirmishes, successfully handled by the Green Jackets and the Hussars, who maintained their good spirits, even in adversity.

As the pursued army approached Torres Vedras, to the amazement of all, fortified lines rose out of the mountains to await them. Wellington's engineers and thousands of Portuguese had built a formidable fortress, trenches, redoubts, gun emplacements, cleared lines of fire and provided adequate supplies. These works, covering all approaches to Lisbon, aided by flotillas of gunboats on the river Tagus, were a miracle of careful planning and showed the genius of Wellington.

Faced by this impregnable obstacle, the French were dumbfounded and, having outrun their communications, could do little else but settle down in a wasted wilderness, with Portuguese guerrillas hampering every movement on the roads behind, a miserable outlook but their master, Bonaparte, would not give up his firm intention to drive the insolent British into the sea. They were unable to go forward and would not go back. But eventually they were obliged, literally by starvation, to pull back to prepared lines at

Santarem, hoping that Wellington would come out and be destroyed; even though the French were subjected to severe weather conditions, a savage hungry army.

Wellington sat tight comfortably supplied by sea, busily planning his movements for the spring of 1811.

6

John and Teresa settled down to a comfortable life, the Marie episode still lurking in the background but little impeding their enjoyment. John knew that in the future, very soon, his services as a courier would be required. They were able to live in style, smart uniforms and gowns. There were balls and much entertainment. Wellington firmly believed in keeping his troops happy and occupied. Training, as always, was relentless, with drill and weapon practice. His oft-quoted advice was that, 'Your horse must be well looked after, but its sole purpose is to get you to the enemy, useless if you cannot fight, arms come first.' Equally true of the infantry man's feet, (a not uncommon practice was to urinate over one's socks and not to change the socks too often), rifles, muskets, bayonets and pistols, immaculate – 'bright, clean and slightly oiled'.

In the early spring of 1811 Wellington himself sent for John.

'Lieutenant, I have a most important task for you,' he said, 'to travel to Fuentes de Oñoro where you will meet Major Murray, as required. Travel with him to Ciudad Rodrigo, returning when the major has completed his despatches. Your success in this mission is vitally important to future operations of my army. Your return should not be after April since by then we shall be on the move northwards.'

John was told that at least he must reach Coimbra, to make his own arrangements for the journey, which would be perilous and, above all, to make his own observations, which he had proved previously to be able to do.

'You may confer with your colonel and squadron leader only, on a need-to-know-basis, and Godspeed,' were

Wellington's farewell words to John.

On his return to the regiment to report to the colonel, a planning meeting was held, just the three officers, to decide the best way to carry out the difficult mission. They decided that the best chance would be, as on a previous occasion, to enlist Teresa and the cart; John to be mentally ill, completely deranged, a merchant from Ciudad Rodrigo who had been operating in Lisbon, not very well treated by the Portuguese, travelling home with his Spanish wife and a servant. Various documents would be arranged to cover the story, business details, address in Lisbon, medical report together with a *passer* from the British on humanitarian grounds.

Teresa was not too enthusiastic but, having agreed, went to work on her part of the preparations, to equip the faithful cart and victual it, buy a new horse and seek a suitable 'servant'. John's horse would be trailing behind and the other man would ride another horse. Teresa quickly found a Spaniard, Leon, an ex-sergeant from the Spanish allied forces, originating from Ciudad Rodrigo, a very willing, able man in his thirties. In two days all was ready and they set off on the coastal track with which they were now familiar to proceed to Mondego, from there to bypass Coimbra over the mountains, skirting Busaco and thence to the rendezvous at Fuentes, just over the border into Spain. The most sensitive part of the journey was the area north of Torres Vedras where the French were maintaining a few divisions, having been obliged to send the bulk of the army to Santarem or into Spain since conditions for them in Portugal were completely inhospitable and hostile. The troops left behind were dispirited and idle and by good fortune the insignificant party on the unfrequented road passed without incident.

The comparatively short journey of some two hundred miles was uneventful, even enjoyable in the early spring weather, with the three of them lying up at night and moving cautiously without noticeable haste. Leon's intimate knowledge of the area guided them safely to Fuentes where they made contact with the major, who warmly greeted his well-known courier and the lovely Teresa. They held a council to plan the immediate operations which highlighted the urgency of getting certain information back to Wellington, a despatch being prepared there and then. It was decided to send Leon, whom they had found to be resourceful and trustworthy, who would travel with all speed with instructions to deliver the message to the general alone, presenting a pass provided by the major when necessary. Thus Wellington would receive early notes of the forthcoming sphere of operations, instead of awaiting the return of John some weeks later; a decisive factor which would enable the planning to be advanced correspondingly.

The major took the role of Leon and by devious movements they moved, using the same cover story, to Ciudad Rodrigo, observing what they could of the French who were much in evidence in the area. Since there was much traffic on the roads they passed into town unnoticed to the safe house. For the next few weeks the major and John gathered much valuable information about the enemy until it was judged the right time to leave with the despatches, attempting to reach Wellington at Torres Vedras.

They planned to travel as before with another loyal servant to Coimbra where they would be taking the stricken John to Teresa's (now Portuguese and married to a Spaniard) mother. At Coimbra, John would go alone, without delay, the hundred miles to the British army, Teresa remaining with her mother at Coimbra.

Travelling by the now very familiar coastal track and crossing the final stage through the French-occupied area by night to arrive safely into the British lines at dawn, John found his way without delay to Lord Wellington. The general was very pleased, confirming the arrival of Leon from Fuentes and most grateful for the precious information from behind the lines.

He told John, 'You have earned a promotion. I will so inform your colonel.'

John's squadron leader was pleased to tell him that he would be made up to captain, and that the promotion was well-deserved. After some thought the major decided that he did not want an extra captain in headquarters' squadron, so John would form a special unit comprising of his old troop and the non-administrative troopers at headquarters; a very useful force. The major told John that, as he must be well-aware from his recent travels, the army would soon be on the move up north and he would meet up with Teresa again.

7

In the spring of 1811 Wellington set out once more northwards, this time to get a foothold in Spain and to stay there. The army was superbly trained and supplied, ready to take on all comers: eight divisions of the British best, confident to defeat Napoleon's troops, they having long lines of communication and hostile surroundings.

John managed a few hours with Teresa at Coimbra, furiously coupling to make up for lost time, as is the way with lusty young soldiers, hot with the prospect of action. Teresa was to remain with her mother until things settled down.

The army pressed forward to Fuentes de Oñoro, occupying the familiar ground with the French drawn up opposite across the shallow stream. The Light Division and the Hussars were placed in reserve behind the centre of the British divisions. At dawn the French marshal attacked the village in strength but was repulsed with heavy losses by the men of the Highland Division, in a furious charge. The fight for Fuentes went on all day and by nightfall it was securely in British hands.

Preparations to establish their lines went on all night and at dawn, the two armies faced each other across the small river. The French moved first, massing opposite the British centre two divisions of cavalry extended over the front and backed up by the three infantry divisions. As they were about to attack, out from the British lines came a battery of the Royal Horse Artillery, galloping hell for leather to a position in front, flanking the French advance. They were superb gunners, probably the best in any army. The guns opened a withering fire into the cavalry now approaching the stream and in range of the British muskets. A stubborn fight ensued for several hours; in the end the bloodied French pulled back, having gained nothing and with many dead and wounded left on the field.

Wellington then decided to attack, bringing the riflemen of the Light Division and the Hussars from their reserve position to attack through the weak point between the facing enemy divisions. The Hussars rode forward into the gap, John's special troop leading in arrow-head formation, and so they passed the gallant Royal Horse Artillery. The guns lumbered up and fell in behind them, artillery charging the enemy. This was too much for the astonished French and John's troop and guns surged through along the Cuidad Rodrigo road, followed by the remainder of the Hussars, the Light Division penetrating and rolling up the flanks of the opposing French. John and the guns pressed on several miles, squashing any opposition from the troops in the rear positions, and established themselves close to the Cuidad Rodrigo road within carbine range with the artillery, in a formidable barrier. Meanwhile, Wellington had set the whole army in a devastating attack along the French front. The French pulled back and finally retreated into the hills on along the Cuidad Rodrigo road. It was a picnic for the dismounted cavalry and the artillery who closed the road, forcing the French into the hills. At this stage of the war the Spanish guerrillas were united in their common hatred of the French, well-armed and a great menace to the enemy moving off the roads. This was a perfect set-up and the French were harassed all the way to Cuidad Rodrigo. It was a very successful battle for the British, determined to stay in Spain, secure in their well-demonstrated superiority in the field. Wellington was well-pleased, particularly with the performance of the Light Division and, of course, the magnificent battery of the Royal Horse Artillery and their unique charge with John's troop of Hussars. The French retired to Cuidad Rodrigo.

In time, the commissariat arrived together with the ladies. Teresa had rejoined the regiment and she and John settled down to a welcome break. The army prepared for the next battle, obviously at Cuidad Rodrigo.

8

Wellington consolidated and reinforced his army in the north, preparing all the summer of 1811 not only for Cuidad Rodrigo but an advance on the capital, Madrid. This was a good time for the army. Wellington believed in plenty of sport and grand balls for the officers. John, now very assured and popular, with a splendid record, and with Teresa (the incident with Marie put aside), everyone enjoyed themselves. Eat, drink and be merry for tomorrow . . .

Meanwhile, in the south, Wellington's other army, commanded by Lord Beresford, kept the French busy. Beresford fought a decisive battle at Albuera and then advanced on Badajoz, a very well-defended fortress town with massive walls. Badajoz was placed under siege and Wellington took charge but in spite of furious onslaughts with many casualties on either side, Badajoz remained in French hands. The advantage gained was that the French moved much of their army to the south, believing that it was there that the British would concentrate their efforts. Wellington seized the opportunity and in January 1812 set about reducing Cuidad Rodrigo, by now having strong defences constructed over the previous months. The British had accumulated a formidable force of artillery which was to be of prime importance in future operations. One particular French redoubt, San Francisco, a very strong position, was the first objective of the British, who poured concentrated artillery fire into the area but meanwhile making a feint attack on an opposite face of the town. Departing from previous tactics, Wellington decided on a night attack on San Francisco. He chose his favourite troops, the hard-worked Light Division, who responded, as ever, in any army when the best are overworked . . . What, not us again . . . !

The silent night attack against the redoubt was a great success. The hammering by the guns for several days had damaged the earthworks and somewhat demoralized the defenders. The riflemen , with the dismounted Hussars, got in among the startled French. After a fierce hand-to-hand fight, the redoubt was taken and Wellington moved up two divisions to consolidate the area, which was close to the town. John and his cavalrymen enjoyed the action, pistols and swords at close quarters: a good scrap with very few casualties. John was run through the arm by a French bayonet: not serious but a wound which would give him a few days with his beloved Teresa.

In the following days the British artillery put up a constant bombardment against the town close to San Francisco and then at dawn, when all was considered timely, the British divisions moved out from the redoubt. The day before the attack on Cuidad Rodrigo, Wellington sent word to the colonel to see him with John Collins. The colonel sent for John, who was recuperating from his wound with Teresa. Wellington congratulated John on his exploits at Fuentes and the magnificent charge with the guns. He went on to tell them that he had a very important job for John: to enter the town right behind the infantry, with his troop, mounted, and to make his way to the French headquarters to capture Marshal Marmont and his staff. The field marshal produced a map of the town, indicating the location of the headquarters which he said that John would probably know following his stay in Cuidad Rodrigo with Major, now Colonel Murray, the exploring officer. Wellington also said that he had just received great news that Napoleon was mobilizing in the east to move against Russia, leaving the British to certain success in Spain.

So John's troop followed closely behind the Light Division, once more in the forefront, and when the outskirts of the town were reached, they passed through the riflemen and brushed aside the resistance from the somewhat stunned enemy and galloped through the streets to the deserted main square and his objective. Dismounting, they stormed into the building, completely surprising the staff who made only token resistance. One colonel drawing his pistol was promptly cut down. Marshal Marmont was absent but they captured General Brennier, an important officer, and most of the staff: a very commendable effort. The colonel was well pleased and sent word to the field marshal of the success of John's raid. The road to Madrid was open and Wellington could see ahead in the coming months: driving the French out of Spain and the British army with a foothold in Spain. But first Badajoz must be taken, a very hard task, it being strongly defended: a fortress with formidable walls. So preparations were made to send all who could be safely spared to the south, while ensuring that Cuidad Rodrigo was not threatened.

9

Following Cuidad Rodrigo, there was little time to rest. Wellington was determined to move against Badajoz when the French were disheartened by the recent defeats and Bonaparte's thoughts were occupied by his plans for the Russian venture.

Wellington sent word for the colonel and John to present themselves forthwith.

The field marshal, addressing John directly, said, 'Captain Collins, you have served me well in the field and on various secret operations. I am much pleased and wish that there were more officers of your calibre. You deserve promotion. Colonel, Collins will be stepped up to major and it is best that he commands the squadron where he is well-known. You can find other duties for the present, squadron leader. The changeover is to be effected when the next operation I have for Collins is completed.' He went on to state the details of the secret operation. 'Colonel Murray is now in Badajoz and you are to join him. It is a very dangerous business and I will instruct Lord Beresford to afford you every assistance. I will be in the south when your job is complete. Report to me alone. Make your own observations and particularly note the locations of the French command as you may be required to repeat your raid on the headquarters at Cuidad Rodrigo. God speed and good luck.'

Back at the regiment it was decided that John should be accompanied by a sergeant and two troopers. Teresa could travel with him. The journey was through friendly country and they could cover the two hundred miles or so in a few days. John consulted with Teresa and they decided to use the cart as the best means of travelling, the soldiers to use a commissariat wagon.

So, well-provisioned, they set off to Coimbra and the well-known coast road, already the main roads were choked with units moving south. Of course, a stopover at Teresa's mother was very convenient. She was delighted to see John, the soldier they had housed, now a splendid young officer. After a pleasant day and night, the company set off for Mondego, Cintra and Lisbon. The journey to Lisbon was uneventful and on arrival they found that General Lord Beresford was at advanced headquarters near Albuera towards Badajoz, another one hundred and fifty miles. On arrival John presented himself to the general with Wellington's orders to assist the venture in every way.

Lord Beresford was in contact with Spanish guerrillas who knew of a secret way into Badajoz, via a concealed tunnel under the wall, dangerous to approach since French outposts surrounded the town. It was clear that John should go in civilian clothes, escorted by his sergeant and troopers and Spanish guides who were to hand. The same evening John said farewell to Teresa who was to remain at headquarters and the small party of civilians set off at dusk to cover the best part of a hundred miles to their destination before which they would leave the horses and proceed on foot. All went well and they reached the jumping-off point from where they would carry on after dark. It was extremely dangerous and very eerie crossing the French lines where they were close enough to hear voices, only encountering one lone soldier relieving himself. He was very quickly despatched by one of the guerrillas.

One guerrilla who also knew how to find Colonel Murray accompanied John into the tunnel. It was before dawn, when people are at their lowest, and the pair passed unchallenged to the colonel's hideout. The colonel was very pleased to see John.

'I am happy that you are here, since I feel that I have been too conspicuous and possibly I am being watched.'

So Colonel Murray told John that the latter would now have to take over, having been briefed on the work done so far, to complete the information about the enemy and the town, particularly possible access over the walls or locations for breaching the defences. It was arranged for the colonel to leave that night with the guide, who would return, and for John to follow in not more than two weeks.

'John, this is the hard one and much depends on the information we provide to the field marshal and to ensure victory in the coming battle.'

John, by now having gained sufficient experience in the game of spying, went about the business inconspicuously, moving always as if going somewhere, not stopping to observe, absorbing what was essential with a quick glance, committing all to memory. Nothing was on paper in case he was arrested. The guide returned and before two weeks were up, they left on the risky journey through the tunnel and the French lines, fortunately without any untoward incident.

On his return, John committed his observations to paper, together with some rough maps. He then contacted Colonel Murray and, together, they went to see Wellington, now at Beresford's headquarters. The field marshal was very happy to receive the information which would greatly assist in the final planning of the imminent storming of Badajoz.

John rejoined his regiment, which was now in the south, and took over the squadron, the ex-squadron leader being found other employment. There was little time to spend with Teresa but they made the most of it, frantic in the light of the impending battle.

10

In mid-March the army commenced digging in the guns in front of Badajoz. All the artillery facing the area of the walls to be breached was just within range, which meant of course, that they were also in range of the few French guns on the wall and, therefore, more of a nuisance than a threat. An infantry division was then engaged in digging trenches close to one of the outlying posts but without musket range. The March weather was cold and wet, providing an unenviable task for the entrenchers.

Towards the end of the month, the breach was beginning in the wall. There was obvious penetration and crumbling and Wellington sent the Light Division into the trenches. At dawn, the riflemen rose from the trenches and stormed the outlying fort. In the ensuing scuffle a third of the riflemen were killed or wounded but finally the enemy gave up. This move, closer to the walls, brought the attack on the breaches more positive. By the first week in April two breaches were made in the walls and the weather was improved. The French general had at once concentrated half the garrison at the breaches, a formidable barrier. The rest were used to make the defences impregnable.

Wellington advanced a night attack, hitherto not favoured, but in the light of recent success in the dark, now considered the only way to approach the awesome breaches. The Light Division was to attack one breach and another infantry division the other. John's squadron, dismounted, was to follow the riflemen and repeat his raid as at Ciudad Rodrigo. It was impossible to use the horses due to the extremely broken ground covered with earthworks and trenches. Meanwhile, another division was to attempt the impossible: escalate the walls, approaching a hundred feet high.

Both the attacking divisions at the breaches were repelled with awful slaughter. The French were almost entirely concentrated there, so the British pulled back. Meanwhile, news was received that, almost miraculously, the division scaling the walls had succeeded and against only slight resistance had gained a foothold inside the walls. This was the spur. The troops at the breaches attacked with ferocious vigour, careless of danger, and surged into Badajoz. That was another step forward to Napoleon's eventual defeat. The soldiers behaved atrociously, raping the women and looting, until stern measures by Wellington's orders put an end to it and restored order.

John, elated in spite of the danger and personal worry, Teresa had told him when they parted that she was with child, set off with the squadron into the town, quickly suppressing any unfortunate French they encountered, arriving at the building where the French staff were, as John knew from his reconnaissance. He ordered the building to be surrounded and with his old troop smashed through the main doors into the hall. The French guards quartered in the hall opened fire and a heavy musket ball hit John squarely in the chest, killing him instantly.

The body was brought out to the British lines and Teresa was informed. She was devastated with grief but consoled by the thought of the child she bore.

John was buried with full military honours, Colonel Murray representing Wellington, who sent his condolences to Teresa on the loss of her husband and a fine soldier.

Part Two
America
1812–1851

11

Shortly after John's funeral the Hussar colonel visited Teresa and spoke about her future. She would, he said, be looked after. Teresa thought that she should go to see John's parents in England and the colonel agreed that this would be satisfactory.

'I will make enquiries as to the next convoy and let you know in good time,' he told her.

Later Teresa was informed that a convoy was leaving from Oporto in two weeks, which was very acceptable as she could visit her mother in Coimbra en route. So it was all arranged and Teresa set off with the cart which had served them so well and had many happy memories. The previous night the officers of the regiment had given her a tremendous farewell dinner. The colonel, in a fond address to Teresa, spoke of her role in assisting John with his various dangerous missions which afforded no small contribution to the successful pursuance of the war, the army would now press on into Spain and the defeat of Napoleon's army.

Teresa travelled to Coimbra with a cavalry escort and was delivered to her mother in style, becoming her status as the widow of a gallant officer. Teresa's mother was saddened by the news of John's death but cheered that Teresa was to have his child. They spent a few comforting days together when Teresa then told her mother that she was going to England to stay with John's family until the baby was born. Pilar was disappointed but agreed that, given the still uncertain outcome in the Peninsula, it would be for the best. They packed Teresa's possessions and valuables, such as she could take on board ship, and together set off in a carriage accompanied by the detachment of Hussars who had been told to see Teresa off with due ceremony.

The journey to Oporto was enjoyable and they arrived in good time to spend a night in an inn, whilst the young officer sent a trooper to locate the vessel, which was due to sail the following day. Arriving at the transport, Teresa said a sad farewell to her mother, Pilar, inside the carriage. Meanwhile, the escort of six troopers dismounted on either side of the gangplank, swords drawn at the salute. The officer accompanied Teresa on board and handed her over to the deck officer. Those on deck were much impressed.

'Who is she? Someone of importance?' they asked.

Teresa was given a small but comfortable single cabin. Soon after, the transport cleared the harbour and joined the others outside; the escorting Royal Navy Frigates shepherding them into formation. It was a fine day, with light wind and sunshine which continued until the convoy was well into the Bay of Biscay.

The third night Teresa was wakened by alarming pitching and tossing of the ship and nearly thrown out of her bunk. Anything loose in the cabin was falling to the floor and clattering about. The Bay had capriciously risen up to a violent storm with south-west Atlantic gale and mountainous rollers. The storm continued for three days and on the third morning, at dawn, the transport was with one other, separated on a vast ocean. Not quite, sailing parallel, was a man-of-war flying the flag of the United States. There was general consternation all round, the transports being unaware that America had declared war on England. The war of 1812 between the US and Britain, 1812-1815, was occasioned by America's resentment over shipping rights enforced by the British and the impressment of American sailors and British sailors serving in their ships. The American navy, including privateers and pirates, somewhat legalized, such as the warship encountered by the transports, was fairly successful. On land, actions on the Canadian border, Lake Erie to Niagara, were indecisive. Finally the British were defeated at New

Orleans and a treaty signed.

The privateer signalled the transports to heave to and when they ignored this, sailing on, fired a warning shot which due to a lurch of the ship or inaccurate aim, did not cross the bow but struck the forepart, causing little damage but instant compliance to stop. Longboats put out from the privateer, with armed sailors and officers, prize crews with orders to embark some of the passengers to make space for them.

The American captain, one Charles Lang, greeted them on the longboats' return and welcomed them on board, explaining that they were technically prisoners of war but would be treated respectfully. The captain spotted the rather outstanding figure of Teresa and was immediately attracted to her. Long at sea without a woman, he was confronted with one very desirable. He arranged quietly with the steward to accommodate her in a single cabin and to see that hers and the others' belongings were fetched from the transports. So the small flotilla sailed on into the Atlantic with fair-weather and comfortable winds.

The captain skilfully insinuated himself into association with Teresa with small favours and attention, which she was well aware of, and of his intentions. Charles Lang was a fine man, tall and broad, not unhandsome, fashioned in the new American way of independence and freedom, attractive to most women, and Teresa also felt a flutter of interest in spite of her so far not obvious pregnancy and recent widowhood.

The fine weather continued and Charles one sunny afternoon invited Teresa to walk with him on the quarterdeck. They exchanged confidences. She told him of her home in Portugal, her first marriage when a young girl and her husband's death by robbers; about John Collins, her second spouse, and their adventures together in the Peninsula and his death in battle. She explained that she had been on her way to see John's parents and made no mention of the unborn child. Charles told her of his home port, Charleston, South Carolina, and of his family home, a large plantation growing cotton and some tobacco, some hundred miles to the north, a wonderful country where his parents still managed the estate which was manned by African slaves.

After their walk and talk, Charles would take her back to her cabin. One afternoon she looked at him with obvious, inviting eyes which asked him not to leave but to come into her quarters. Charles was not loath and they crowded into the cramped space, bodies inevitably touching.

Teresa said, 'Charles, I am a few weeks with child but quite excited by the atmosphere and the motion of the ship. Should you wish, you may take me but, please, not too vigorously as I do not wish to lose the baby.'

Charles's response was to take her in his arms and kiss her passionately, his hands fondling her breasts and cupping her buttocks. She raised her voluminous skirt and untied the waistband of her drawers, stepping back so that they dropped to the floor, turned and faced down on the bunk revealing lovely twin globes of satiny flesh and long shapely legs, the moist, inviting orifice readily exposed. He inserted his substantial member slowly into Teresa, moving without haste in and out as she had desired, agonizingly, tormentingly, resisting the need to thrust more quickly until at last they climaxed together – a shattering explosion. Charles did not withdraw and after a short pause commenced the movement again to arrive at a very satisfactory ending for both.

They stood clasping each other with great joy and he said, 'I love you very much, darling Teresa. I hope that we shall be happy together.'

For two more weeks the ship and prizes sailed on without incident. The lovers were infatuated with each other and enjoyed their amorous encounters in either of their quarters, Charles's being roomier and affording them more scope for their lovemaking.

On arrival at Charleston they were greeted with cheers by

the onlookers at the quayside. Not often did two prizes arrive after one venture. Word spread and crowds gathered to watch the ships tied up and to welcome the captain when he stepped ashore.

Charles had discussed his and Teresa's immediate future and now arranged to acquire a small town house and an indoor servant. Neither was short of funds and the arrangements were very satisfactory.

Three weeks passed easily. Charles had visited his parents at the plantation and on his return he informed Teresa that he would have to leave shortly on another voyage which would mean several months of absence from her.

He said, 'I will always love you and on my return will ask you to marry me. Meanwhile, I wish you all the best for the birth of your child as I am sure to be absent then.'

When Charles left, Teresa settled down comfortably in her cosy house well looked after by her African maid who was a freed slave, given her liberty by an English family whom she had served for ten years who had left for England at the outbreak of war. Consequently, the woman, who had papers establishing her free status, was very contented, especially as she was now paid a wage. By good fortune, Teresa's nearest neighbours were a Spanish émigré family who had left when the French entered Madrid. They had formed a group with others who were also refugees from Spain and Teresa was made welcome to their society. Teresa wrote a letter, to be carried by a neutral ship, to John's parents at the North End Farm, explaining that the ship on which she had been travelling to see them had been captured by an American warship and now she was far away across the Atlantic. She told them about the coming child and, whilst officially a prisoner of war, she was not under restraint and had been amply assisted by her captor, one Captain Lang. Consequently, she had elected to stay until the child was born.

Under happy circumstances, well cared for and with good friends, the weeks passed very quickly and the time arrived for taking to childbed. Without any problems the child was born, a boy whom she had already decided to baptize Juan Collins, and so it was.

Charles had told his parents about the lovely widow, whom he had captured on his last voyage, but nothing of their present relationship. As he had suggested to Teresa, she wrote to them that she would like to visit the captain's parents as she was now delivered of her child and would be able to make the journey in a few weeks' time. In due course a reply came that she would be welcome. Ridgeway, where the plantation was situated, was a few miles north of the state capital, Columbia, and easy to find. The Oaks was well known.

When Juan was three months old, Teresa decided that they could travel to Ridgeway and sent a message that she would be arriving soon. A small coach was hired and, accompanied by the servant, they set off on the two-day journey, stopping en route at an inn. Teresa was delighted with the lush countryside as they passed rivers and lakes, quiet villages and grand plantations, mostly growing cotton but some with tobacco. It was all very prosperous.

The Oaks, situated after a mile drive through the plantation, amazed Teresa with its magnificence. It was a splendid porticoed colonial-style mansion. Charles's parents were very welcoming, expressing their regrets at her recent loss and forced removal to a foreign country. Teresa assured them that their son, Charles, had been very kind and sympathetic. They were delighted with little Juan and said that she was welcome to stay as long as she wished. In fact, Charles, who had been away for many months, should be home soon.

During her stay, Teresa told of her home life, her two marriages which had ended in tragedy, and her decision to visit her late husband's home. They were astonished by Teresa's part in the war, involved as she had been in dangerous, secret missions with her soldier husband. They sensed from Teresa's casual remarks about their son that there was more between the pair than just friendship.

Teresa thoroughly enjoyed riding around the estate with Charles's father, observing that the slaves appeared to be content and well looked after, as was necessary in order to get the most out of them. Of course, the one important factor that was missing in their lives was freedom. The only way they could move away was if they were sold to another plantation and this caused them great sorrow, coupled with missing their native Africa. The neighbours were delighted to meet Teresa and listen to her adventurous story. Great parties were held, as was the custom in the southern states.

12

As Charles' parents predicted, he arrived one day, breezing in with a tang of the sea, over-jubilant from a successful voyage. The parents were surprised at the enthusiasm with which he greeted Teresa but not altogether so. They suspected something was afoot.

Charles was delighted with Juan and when the pair were alone said, 'Teresa, as I told you before I left, I hope that you will marry me. I love you and will regard Juan as my own, which might very well have been so.'

Teresa said that it was her dearest wish and so they went to tell the parents, who were also delighted. Charles announced that he intended to swallow the hook and and so had informed the authorities that he proposed to live on the plantation and to help his parents. Charles's mother and father were delighted as they were getting old and needed the help he would afford. The happy couple set off for Charleston to clear up their affairs and to close Teresa's house. They were delighted that they could now make unrestricted love, which they performed enthusiastically and frequently.

On their return, arrangements for the wedding were put in hand and they were congratulated by the community, except for their immediate neighbours. Soon after their return the neighbours' son arrived, confronting Charles.

He struck him on the face saying, 'You have dishonoured my sister, avowing your intentions to marry her. I will meet you tomorrow at daybreak on the bridge which divides our properties.'

Charles had no choice but to accept and assured his parents and Teresa that he was quite capable with a pistol, which he was challenged with and had elected to use. He arranged for an old friend to act as his second and went to bed with Teresa untroubled.

They met at the bridge at daybreak and adjourned to a level open space nearby where the principal presented a case of duelling pistols, saying, 'Check that they are loaded.'

The duellists took up the position indicated, standing back to back moving apart on the count, commencing and, at twenty paces, turning and firing. Charles's opponent fell and, upon examination by the attending surgeon, was found to be dead, shot through the heart. The bullet fired at Charles passed between his left arm and chest, penetrating his clothing and lacerating his ribs: nothing serious. The end of the affair was that the neighbours sold up and went away to avoid further inevitable feuding: a satisfactory ending. All were so relieved that Charles was forgiven for his behaviour.

The wedding was a grand affair, attended by most of the local society, plantation owners and state officials, held in the small church at Ridgeway which was crowded. Juan was in the care of his surrogate grandmother. Some wondered but most knew the story of his origin. A lavish reception was held at the house and the newly-weds departed with much cheering and good will from the guests for a week at the parents' town house in Columbia which was always kept ready and staffed.

On their return, Charles began to take over some of the running of the plantation and Teresa, likewise, interested herself in the household and associated affairs, welcomed by her new mother with whom she got on very well.

13

Trade was flourishing in spite of the war against England. Other outlets were sought. Cotton was much in demand and, of course, tobacco. The Napoleonic wars were coming to a close. The British had entered metropolitan France along the southern borders.

Among the plantation owners there was much talk of expansion but the available lands were in the hands of the native Indians. It was the beginning of the obvious solution – to move the Indians westward to unoccupied territory, of which there was an abundance in the middle west. So germinated the start of the Indian Wars, approved by the government, to erupt in a few years' time.

Life on the plantation was peaceful and very rewarding. After a few years, Charles's parents decided to retire to the town house in Columbia, leaving the management to their son, who had proved very able at the running of things.

Juan was growing and it was time to think of his education. Enquiries in Columbia led them to a young Englishwoman who had stayed on at the end of the war and was now free from a similar position with a well-known family. Miss Jane Brown accepted the position offered. She was well-suited, Teresa considered, to take on Juan. Jane was well-spoken, capably educated, obviously respectable, plain looking but not unattractive, unmarried since her fiancé had been killed in the Peninsula, therefore having a common bond with Teresa. Juan took to Jane and, as she was a good teacher, became an intelligent pupil, quick to absorb the basics of an education that was to stand him in good stead. He had a particular friend, the son of a neighbour,

Roger Russell, and together they learned to ride, use firearms, to hunt in the forests, swim and sail at a nearby lake. Teresa also cared for his appearance, cleanliness and dress and, altogether, he grew up a fine boy.

Teresa's old maid from Charleston decided that it was time to retire and, having saved enough money, said that she would go to live among friends in that city. Teresa found a replacement for her, a young nubile girl, quite personable and attractive, with a light brown complexion, whom she herself would train to serve her as she wished from a personal maid.

Teresa sometimes went off to Columbia to see Charles's parents and to shop for such things as clothes, perfumes and cosmetics, and various other items for her men. One day during her absence Juan, after lunch, was going up to his bedroom. The house still and quiet with everyone resting, he heard muffled noises coming from his parents' bedroom. The door carelessly being left ajar, he peered in and there on the bed, quite naked, he saw his father on top of Miss Jane, thrusting away vigorously. As he watched, with little cries from Miss Jane, the movement stopped and Juan crept away, very disturbed. He had seen animals performing the same act and, at fourteen years, had experienced sexual stirrings, ejaculating whilst asleep and also by his own hand, very normal for boys of his own age. Roger, his friend, confessed to similar activities. Juan's thoughts turned to girls and he conceived a lustful desire for Teresa's maid who was certainly a suitable subject to approach, particularly as he had noticed her paying attention to him with a certain glance from her eyes.

One afternoon he chanced to meet her on the upstairs corridor, and taking her hand led her willingly on her part to an unused bedroom where they embraced. The girl, sensing Juan's inexperience, undressed him, taking his already stiffened penis in her hand until it was almost bursting. Quickly slipping off her clothes she laid down on the bed and spread her legs, pulling Juan down on top of her and guiding him into her welcoming vagina. It was over very quickly. He came, accompanied by great shuddering gasps and lay still. As his organ did not subside he recommenced the movement until they erupted together in a glorious orgasm.

This happy amorous affair continued for several months until the inevitable occasion when Teresa, who was serenely happy with an unexpected pregnancy came across Charles embracing a weeping Miss Jane. Teresa was furiously angry, especially when she found out that Miss Jane was, like herself, several months with child, most certainly of Charles' making.

Teresa said to them, 'Charles, I will speak to you later, and you, hussy, come to my office now.'

Miss Jane was ordered to leave forthwith and advised to return to England. Teresa would see that she and the child were provided for and gave her sufficient money to carry her along for such time until other arrangements could be made. She was thinking of the farm and John Collins's parents, who might be able to help without knowing the truth of the affair. So that same day Miss Jane departed.

Teresa's perception was aroused by the discovery of what had been going on in her own house. She forgave Charles, accepting that he had in her absence been seduced. However, she quite suddenly became aware that her maid was also showing signs of pregnancy. Questioning the girl achieved nothing. She would not reveal who the father was. Teresa considered the possibilities. The girl rarely left the house and in a sudden flash of intuition, she realized that it was Juan and so it proved. He admitted responsibility. Well, what a shake-up in the family: two erring males and so many pregnancies. The maid was sent back to the slaves' quarters, with assurances that she would be taken care of, and Teresa looked for a new personal servant, one who wouldn't invite sexuality.

Then there was the problem of Juan's education. In any case, it had progressed to the limit of Miss Jane's ability.

Discussing this, they decided that as Charles was a graduate of Harvard University, he should write to the dean of faculty, explaining that Juan was prepared for university and could he be considered for entry as a student to Harvard? The letter added two years to Juan's age, being the right one at seventeen, and also included his friend, Roger, with the Russells' consent.

The reply was encouraging. It said, in gist, yes, send the young men for interview and, if acceptable, they can be admitted to the university forthwith. I look forward to greeting them.

Juan and Roger were readied for the journey and it was assumed that they would be staying at Harvard and would return in some months for the vacation. Fond farewells were said and the plantation settled down peacefully following the pregnancies' trouble, Teresa to await the birth of another son, or so she was convinced.

The journey northwards was an eye-opener, neither Juan nor Roger had travelled further than Columbia and they were astonished by the vastness of the country and its natural wealth. They were, as expected, found suitable to enter the university as undergraduates.

14

Life at Harvard was very full, apart from study, for which they both chose history, there were games, parties, inevitable drinking, often to excess and relieving visits to one of the many whorehouses, much better than dallying with the young ladies they met at balls. Vacation time arrived all too soon and their homecoming was a welcome change. Juan who had grown both in stature and intellect, was a very handsome young man and was so like his father that Teresa wept for the past and John, although very contented with Charles and Juan's newly born half-brother, as she predicted the child would be. Juan made discreet enquiries about his first love and was told that she had given birth to a lovely girl and was very happy and well cared for via Teresa. Juan sent presents but wisely refrained from seeing her.

After three years the finals were taken and they both passed with satisfactory degrees, albeit not first-class but then they had not over-worked, there being too many more engaging activities.

The Indian Wars had been going on since 1820 and would continue for twenty-five years. The plantation owners and farmers wanted fertile lands to the east presently occupied by the native Indians and the government backed them up by designating an area known as the Indian territory situated in the prairie land of Oklahoma from the Red River northwards. The tribes, were mainly Cherokee, who were quite militant, and also minor groups. Creek, Senivole, Choctaw, and Chickasaw. The Indians were obviously unwilling to move and resisted force so that in effect a considerable war ensued which lasted for quite a few years.

Other Indian tribes joined in and eventually the fighting spread as far as Colorado and Arizona; desert country somewhat inhospitable. The US cavalry were employed in the conflict and became the elite of the army.

The boys now eighteen and having heard much about the war, decided they would like to join the army and being southerners and good horsemen would try for commissions in the cavalry. Juan's parents were not very enthusiastic, but as they had another son and Teresa was again expecting, agreed that as it was more convenient than West Point, he should go to the Citadel Military College.

During a year at college they were instructed in army lore, traditions, drills, swordsmanship, shooting, map reading and other relevant matters. On passing out the principal provided them with letters of introduction to the commandant of the cavalry depot, recommending them as suitable material. Juan's interview was most successful: a student of Harvard and the Citadel, father an officer of Hussars, killed in action at Badajoz during the Peninsular War, he was accepted for a commission as second lieutenant, as was Roger. They were to spend some weeks at the depot to complete their training and be readied for posting to a field regiment.

With others, newly joined, they were put under instruction with a young captain fresh from the west and en route to a staff course. The captain was a typical young blood of the south, son of a gentleman, brought up as a sportsman, a brave, fine rider, bold and dangerous to tangle with, caring only for a good horse and open country; a first-rate shot, flamboyant in dress and mannerisms, in other words, perfect cavalry material.

In a few weeks they were considered ready to enter the field. Juan, Roger and two other officers were to go west with a body of some thirty replacements, among them old troopers returning to their regiments. Each individual was equipped to be self-sufficient. Apart from weapons, each had his own bed roll, personal items, and a few days' food and water. Each rider carried also one half of a two-man bivouac. The journey of some one thousand five hundred miles would take several weeks, crossing through, Georgia, Alabama, Mississippi, Arkansas, Oklahoma and across the Red River to Fort Worth in Texas. They would sleep rough out in the open and replenish supplies from military depots. At weekly intervals, halts of two days would allow the horses to rest and the men to wash clothes and make and mend.

15

The journey emphasized the vastness of America and its ever-changing scenery, quite overwhelming to those who had not travelled further than their home states. From Atlanta, Georgia, they would join the South West trail, a route which the settlers took to Arizona and the fertile South Carolina, the beginning of territory likely to be hostile. There were roving bands of Indians to be encountered, those resisting settlement in the Indian Territory of Oklahoma.

All went well until one night when they were awakened by the sound of a shot coming from the area where the horses were tethered. Men sent to the horse lines found the two sentries dead, with their skulls split open. One had obviously fired his carbine as he fell. A few horses were gone.

Before dawn the men were ready to move out when a scout returned to say that the way to the trail was blocked by Indians. As daylight grew they could see a group of mounted tribesmen about one hundred strong. The officer in command decided to attack and they moved out into the open, forming line extended, and moved towards the hostiles who were within musket shot. The Indians had a few muskets and fired indiscriminately, unfortunately hitting the officer who was, as customary, leading the formation. He fell dead and Juan, who was nearest, galloped to the lead. They advanced into the Indians, swords thrusting and plunging, a ferocious mêlée. The Indians were no match for the disciplined, well-trained troopers and broke away and fled, leaving half their number dead or wounded. The cavalry had sustained the officer and three troopers dead. They buried them with a small ceremony, formed up and rode on accompanied by the horses which had been stolen. By custom, they rejoined the formation they had been used to and familiar horses. By consent, Juan took over command. From then on they proceeded without further aggression from the tribes but did observe several bands out of range and not showing any hostility.

They arrived at Red River and crossed into Texas over a ford where horses could walk except in the centre, when both horse and rider had to swim, the man clinging to the horse's bridle. At Fort Worth they reported to the commandant informing him of the clash with the Indians and the loss of an officer and his troopers. They were told to rest and that they would be posted to a patrol headquarters just across the river in the south of Oklahoma. So they crossed the river again, located the patrol camp and were welcomed by a captain who commanded two patrol units which covered part of the trail to the west. They were much subjected to harassment by the Indians who burnt and looted caravans and slaughtered the unfortunate settlers. There were two patrols which operated alternatively. Juan and Roger were to command a troop each in the same patrol unit which was led by a senior lieutenant.

The patrols were out for two weeks at a time covering an area of some three hundred miles along the trail. Juan's patrol encountered no incident with the Indians for several months and then ran into a big one. Smoke was sighted some way ahead, too much for a camp fire. Proceeding at a fast pace, they saw eventually a circle of wagons, the customary procedure for a night stop and the settlers must have been surprised at dawn. The camp was surrounded by tribesmen firing into the wagons as they rode round. Little return fire was coming from the settlers and many wagons were blazing. Some Indians had vaulted their horses into the circle and obviously the slaughter would soon be over.

The cavalry galloped to the scene, quickly breaking up the circle of Indians who turned to give fight but were somewhat dismayed by the sudden appearance of the soldiers. Juan's troop entered the circle through a gap between the wagons and set about the Indians rampaging inside. It was soon over. None were left alive. One trying to escape with a young woman was cut down by Juan who dismounted and went to the girl, who was lying in a faint. She came to in Juan's arms, shaking from the horrors she had seen, but reassured by the presence of the army, quickly recovered. Meanwhile, outside, the Indians had fled, leaving many dead behind. The cavalry followed, catching up with a few stragglers who were dealt with.

Few of the settlers were left alive and the Indians had taken most of the horses at the outset, so it was decided to take only three serviceable wagons and send them back to the patrol camp. The girl, who was named Mary Skinner, approached Juan to thank him. She had lost her parents and was very distraught. Juan comforted her and suggested that she should go to Fort Worth where she would be looked after and maybe they would meet there when the patrol returned.

The settlers left and the cavalry, who had suffered only two fatal casualties in the fight, continued the patrol without further incident and returned to the camp to rest. The settlers had decided to wait on the trail and join another caravan. A few, who had had enough, went to Fort Worth, including Mary who secretly thought that she would see Juan there. She was not only grateful to him but quite attracted to the handsome young officer.

The patrols continued with only minor incidents, but meeting up with other units at the boundary of their area, they learnt of equally horrifying attacks on the migrants, similar to their own recent experience. The tour was soon over and when they were relieved were glad to return to the relative civilization of Fort Worth where there was a mess for officers and good canteen facilities for the men, with quite considerable drunkenness, as one might expect.

Juan found Mary Skinner who was making herself useful at the post school run by the padre. Mary was very grateful to Juan and they enjoyed each other's company, managing to take walks outside the Fort in the desert, with no danger from natives, exchanging their stories, Mary, fresh out from England, was enthralled by his account of his father killed in Spain, his Portuguese mother and life on the plantation, Harvard and the army.

Obviously they became very fond of each other and when the time came for Juan's unit to return to the prairie, all too soon, they embraced fervently, Juan telling Mary, 'When I return I will ask you something very important.'

They arrived back at the patrol camp and the routine of guarding the trail kept them on the move, mostly without any major incident, until one day they came across a caravan, wagons burnt and looted, horses gone, many corpses which had been scalped: a gruesome sight. Having with them an experienced tracker it was decided to follow the fresh trail since it appeared from those bodies remaining that some of the women and girls had been carried off. They pressed on for some days, carefully scouting ahead, until word was sent back that the Indian village had been sighted and from the trail it was surely the one they were seeking. They lay up overnight, intending to attack at first light, hopefully undetected. The dawn is always a time of lax vigilance.

The lieutenant sent two dismounted troopers to approach the village to observe any activity or sentries and to report back before dawn. They were also to report on the terrain, obstacles or ditches. The troopers returned saying that all was quiet, the village sleeping and the going good.

At first light they moved off at a walk, as quietly as possible. As soon as they were close enough they saw movement. They had been seen and the village came to life, with braves pouring out of wigwams. The cavalry broke into a canter. The extended line pressing forward at either end enclosed half the village, like the horns of a buffalo. One section had been detailed to find the horses and drive them off, preventing any escape. The troopers were now into the village, slashing away at the Indians with their swords and downing many. Under the circumstances, men on foot have an advantage over those mounted. The braves responded furiously, knowing that it was a fight to the death, their death. With tomahawk and lance they brought down some of the horses, despatching their riders. Eventually, all the braves were killed or wounded. The dismounted troopers cleared the wigwams of the squaws, some fighting and clawing like cats. The whites, some seventy women, were released from a large tent in a very sorry state. Taking stock, they appraised many casualties of their own lying dead or wounded, among them Roger Russell, impaled by a lance, quite dead. Juan was on his feet clutching his left arm which was found to be practically severed from the blow of a tomahawk. He was in a sorry state.

They drove off the squaws and set fire to the village, after recovering some wagons which could transport the wounded and the women unable to ride. It was a successful but costly operation and the survivors were quite saddened by the losses. The wounded were cared for by two troopers skilled in rough doctoring. It was obvious that Juan's arm would have to be amputated but they forbore to do so, strapping it up as best they could. Fortunately, the main artery was intact and the bleeding was controlled.

Back at the advance camp, the wounded were given further first aid and, with the released women, sent off to Fort Worth. Juan was suffering from severe shock and it was essential that he received attention quickly or he would not recover. At Fort Worth the wounded were put in the field hospital where the two resident surgeons went to work. Juan's left arm was cut off above the elbow and he was in a comatose state for several days, quite miraculously regaining consciousness eventually.

Mary, of course, knew that he was in hospital and called frequently to enquire about him and was relieved when told that he was conscious and that she could pay a brief visit to his bedside.

As Juan recovered sufficiently to take an interest in his surroundings, Mary said to him, 'What were you going to ask me? You said that you were going to say something when you came back here.'

Juan replied that he loved her and was going to ask her to marry him but now, maybe, she would not want a one-armed man for a husband.

Mary replied indignantly, 'Of course, I will marry you. I love you too and the sacrifice of your arm makes you even dearer to me.'

As Juan grew better he was able to take walks with Mary and they planned for their future and the wedding. He would be sent to the east to a military hospital to check the surgery done to his arm and to completely recover. It was decided that Mary would go to his parents to wait for him, which should not be long as he was, in fact, feeling very well. His stump, although painful, had healed well and fortunately was not septic.

They left together by military transport, well-guarded through the hostile area until, without incident, they arrived at Atlanta. Juan was duly hospitalized and Mary set off for the plantation with a letter from Juan explaining the circumstances, knowing that his parents would welcome her.

At the hospital the surgeon examined Juan, commenting that a good job had been carried out on the arm, which only needed a little trimming. He was to remain at the hospital for a few weeks, in case of complications, and also to restore his general physical condition.

Mary was made most welcome by Teresa and Charles at the plantation. They approved Juan's choice of a future wife. Mary was introduced to the neighbours, much entertained and shown round the county. She also spent a week with Juan's grandparents in Columbia. She was most impressed. What she was now experiencing, the wealth and high society, was much more than she had imagined, coming from a very ordinary, albeit respectable, background. In spite of the tragic loss of her parents being still fresh in her thoughts, she felt very content with her prospects as Juan's wife.

16

Juan's return home was joyous. His mother and father were delighted to have him back but sorrowful over his infirmity which Juan said, in fact, made little difference. He could still ride, only mounting was a little ungainly with one arm.

The round of social visits started all over and preparations for the wedding were begun. The happy couple got to know each other and to become very much in love. With admirable restraint, Juan refrained from consummating their engagement, delaying sexual union until after the marriage out of respect for Mary: quite an admirable feat on his part.

The wedding took place in Ridgeway followed by a grand reception at the plantation. Afterwards, the newly-weds departed for a honeymoon in New York. The wedding night was celebrated at an inn en route, Mary losing her virginity without much trouble, and both were to find great pleasure in their sex life. Mary proved to be most enthusiastic. All too soon they returned from their idyllic holiday, with Juan due to report to the depot.

The commandant welcomed Juan back, commiserated with him on his loss and remarked that his commanding officer had given him a very good report. There was no reason why he should not continue in the army, probably with promotion. Juan requested a year's leave in order to visit his grandparents in England. His request was granted, on half-pay.

Returning home, he told Mary and his parents of his one year's leave of absence and his plan to visit his father's home in England. They very much approved, especially as Teresa had been prevented from doing so by the war, and Charles.

Charles's contacts in Charleston would assist them in obtaining a suitable passage.

Provided with ample funds by Charles, the plantation flourishing and money plentiful, they left for Charleston where Charles's letter of introduction found them a swift passenger ship plying to Liverpool.

The weather was enjoyable, the sea moderate and for the first week or so the passengers were delighted with the experience, new to most of them. The young couple were very popular, particularly as Juan was a wounded hero fresh from fighting those awful Indians and Mary was orphaned by them: a romantic story. The motion of the vessel and the excitement of the voyage caused Mary to feel very amorous and Juan was very willing to accommodate her. In spite of the cramped conditions, or perhaps because of them, they achieved some remarkable couplings in undreamed of positions.

On they sailed in harmony with the elements until they were aroused one night by the violent motion of the ship and the crash of falling objects. On deck, the wind was of hurricane force, the seas mountainous. Sails were trimmed to maintain headway only. The passengers were battened in and many became seasick. Juan and Mary clung together, anticipating the end at any moment. For three days the storm raged and then capriciously died down so that they were almost becalmed. The passengers were allowed on deck where they were to find a ghastly mess of tangled cordage, broken yards, rigging and spars. Only limited canvas could be used, the ship barely making headway. Below, all worked to clean things up and the galley got going. All were feeling relieved to have survived the storm, grateful to be alive.

The vessel limped into Donegal on the west coast of Ireland. The captain informed the passengers that urgent repairs were necessary as the crossing of the Irish Sea could be rough. The delay would be about one week and passengers could go ashore.

Juan and Mary decided to go on by coach, to see Ireland

and eventually catch the ferry from Dublin to Fishguard. They found Ireland amazingly green, with beautiful lakes and streams. The Irish were friendly and charming but dreadfully poor and frequently appeared to be half-starved, the land being insufficient to feed the population who were also shamefully exploited by the landowners and the aristocracy. Nevertheless, they found it all very enjoyable and after three lively weeks reached Dublin where they spent a few days.

The boat to Fishguard was crowded. Many Irish people were seeking work in England. The voyage was uneventful and without delay Juan and Mary took the coach to London, which city Mary had visited before from her home in Northampton.

They stayed for a few days at a hotel which Mary knew, to rest and see the sights and buy new outfits so that they would arrive at the Collins's farm in good order. They took a private coach to Hampstead, some six miles out of town, and down to North End Village and the farm. They were made most welcome by Juan's grandparents who were so thrilled at last to meet the son of their John whose death in the Peninsula had caused them much sorrow. Juan told them about the plantation in South Carolina, Harvard and the Indian Wars and how he rescued Mary from the Indians. Charles Dickens was staying at the farm, which was commodious with sufficient bedrooms for several guests. He was recovering from the death of his well-beloved sister-in-law, Mary Hogarth. In fact, Dickens often stayed there, finding the peaceful country atmosphere helpful in writing his novels. William Collins, Juan's grandfather, was very well-known and respected so various people of note, including the painter, his namesake, William Collins, and later on his son, Wilkie Collins the novelist, as well as John Linnel and William Blake were also guests. The farmhouse contained a splendid oak-panelled bedroom which his grandfather said that Juan and Mary could have when Dickens left.

One day Mary told Juan that she was going to have a child.

Of course, he was delighted, especially as it could be born in England and have dual nationality. Equally startling to Juan was coming face-to-face with a visitor to the house – none other than his erstwhile governess, Miss Jane; indeed an extraordinary surprise for both of them. Teresa had arranged for Miss Jane on her return from America to go to Juan's grandparents whom she had written to ask them to help her. Miss Jane was now in charge of a small church school in the village which had been built for a wealthy family of the local gentry who were into brewing and banking and also very religious. The school also functioned as a church. Although unconsecrated, and full Sunday services were held, there were no baptisms, weddings or funerals, these being a function of the Hampstead Parish Church. She was living in one of a row of cottages belonging to the farm and adjacent to the church school, very happy and grateful for Teresa's help. Perhaps fortunately, she had lost Charles's ill-conceived child during a violent storm on her passage across the Atlantic arriving at the farm in a sorry state, which was explained by the ordeal of the journey. She was soon to recover her health. Juan and Mary were, of course, frequent visitors to her cottage.

Juan, thinking of the future in a sedentary activity suited to his injury, thought that he could usefully study the role of bailiff or agent and understudy the very experienced farm bailiff who took care of the administration, workers, servants, wages, the farm buildings and cottages in the village and all kinds of supplies and equipment; all those administrative duties other than the actual farming. Juan had in mind his future employment in the army and later, perhaps, on the plantation, or as things were shaping-up, plantations. William Collins agreed and promised to help him in this venture, adding that Juan might gain experience in banking at the local branch in Hampstead where the manager was a great friend of his. So Juan occupied himself usefully whilst Mary helped with the house and also visited her aunt and uncle at Northampton. She spent some weeks there. She had so much to tell of her amazing adventures, unbelievable to people who barely left their own homes. Visits were also paid to other relatives and friends in the vicinity. Mary felt that it was unlikely that she would ever return and so said goodbye and returned to the farm.

All too quickly time passed. Mary gave birth to a son who was christened John Collins, after his grandfather, at a splendid ceremony held at the parish church. Juan's year's leave was coming to an end and one month before it did he left for America with some anxiety about taking little John on such an arduous journey. All went well and they arrived home, with the new addition causing much excitement. Teresa and Charles were overjoyed with their grandson, who was also taken to meet his great-grandparents in Columbia He was by now a much travelled baby.

Meanwhile, Juan reported to the depot and it was arranged that he would be employed in the headquarters commissariat, with the rank of captain. He could find suitable accommodation for his family who would be welcome on the post. Juan proved very able at the job, due probably to his year of coaching in administrative matters at the farm, and after one year he became a very young major, much to Mary's delight and, of course, his parents'. Mary paid frequent visits to the plantation where little John, growing into a fine boy, was spoilt by all.

It would not be long before John, or Johnny as he was nicknamed to avoid confusion, would need schooling. Teresa was, quite naturally, against a governess. Juan had told her about Miss Jane and her good fortune, due to Teresa's request to the Collinses, and suggested that his mother could cope until he could go to a school, possibly in Columbia, where his great-grandparents could keep an eye on him.

17

Juan's proficiency in supply activities was appreciated by his superior officers and, quite unexpectedly, after only two years' service as a major he was made up to lieutenant-colonel and given command of an advance ammunition and arms depot situated on the outskirts of Atlanta, Georgia. Their circumstances were now much improved. They took a fine house in the town and had a sufficiency of servants, a good social life, and Johnny could attend a junior school which was set up for the children of the upper classes.

They remained in Atlanta for five years. The boy had been sent to his great-grandparents in Columbia who, although of advanced age, were able to take care of him. Juan's parents, whom they occasionally were able to visit, were now middle-aged and not so active and he realized that the time had come to join them on the plantation which had been enlarged considerably by the acquisition of neighbouring properties. The Indian Wars were less of a problem as the tribes were being forced into the allotted Indian Territories, so that when Juan requested his release from the army it was granted, albeit reluctantly.

Juan's parents were delighted. It was true that they needed more help and, of course, Juan, at just over thirty years of age, was very vigorous and active, besides being well-experienced in being in charge of things. Johnny was doing well at school, growing up into a fine youth but somewhat wild when away from school. Life on the plantation was busy but very enjoyable, with many functions and parties. Juan, although very popular with the ladies, resisted any attempt to involve himself in an extramarital affair, being very happy in his family life with Mary who had borne him two more children, boy and girl. Juan's half-brother had turned out to be a wild one and had long since departed to the far west, presumably to California.

In due course, Johnny was ready for Harvard University and entry was facilitated as Juan and Charles were both graduates. His sojourn there was just two years. He became too fond of the good life and was too popular with the ladies, culminating in a disastrous affair. For some months he had been having a serious involvement with a young, very attractive, married woman at her house, unsuspected by the husband, until one afternoon he came home, finding the house apparently deserted, then becoming aware of lovemaking noises coming from upstairs; the rhythmic creak of bedsprings and small cries. Quietly he made his way to the bedroom, flung open the door and there, quite naked, were the couple; his wife on top of Johnny and obviously about to reach a climax. Screaming, the wife scrambled off Johnny to the opposite side of the bed but too late for him to stop his erect member ejaculating spurts of his juice. Nevertheless, he sprang to his feet and faced the enraged husband who was throwing wild punches at him. Johnny, a tough young man used to brawling, clasped his hands tightly together, arms raised, bringing them down like a club and hitting the poor man on his forehead, following up with another shattering blow which felled him to the floor, flat on his back and unconscious.

The erstwhile lovers were horrified. Hurriedly dressing, they lifted her husband on to the bed and loosened his clothing. He was barely breathing and the girl said, 'I must send for a doctor. I will invent a story of an intruder who raped me and attacked my husband. You must go quickly. It is sad that it has ended like this. I will send word to you tomorrow.'

The next morning he received a message via a servant.

'My husband is still unconscious and is expected to die. You must leave here at once as they will be searching for the villain,' it said.

With a sad heart, Johnny made arrangements to leave after informing the dean that he had to go home on urgent family business. He vowed to himself never to use the vicious double-fisted blow which he had picked up from the rough house doorman of a saloon. In fact, he vowed to refrain altogether from brawling.

His return to the plantation was a cause for concern, more so when, without going into details, he told his parents that he had seriously injured or possibly killed a man in self-defence. Teresa and Charles were quite horrified and overnight decided with Juan and Mary that Johnny should at once leave for England and continue his education there, first going to his great-grandparents at the farm. The matter was made easier as Johnny was now a wealthy young man, having inherited from his great-grandparents who had both died the previous year, within weeks of each other.

At Charleston, accompanied by Juan, a ship was conveniently leaving in two days and father and son parted sorrowfully for what turned out to be several years. The Atlantic crossing was without complications by the weather and he arrived at North End Village in much better heart, being young and quickly burying the unpleasant affair.

Part Three

England and the Crimea

1851–1856

18

Johnny, although unexpected was, of course, made most welcome. His story was that it was considered desirable for him to complete his education at an English university. William Collins was now quite old and his son, James, the brother of John who was killed in the late wars, was running the farm, which in fact was presently not prospering, the result of bad weather and poor harvests for several years and insufficient funds. Johnny quickly grasped the situation and said that he could help and, with his parents' consent, providing the necessary monies to restore affairs. Meanwhile, he enlisted his great-grandfather's help to use his quite considerable influence to get him a place at Oxford.

He found the life at the farm, the village and the countryside very enjoyable. Many of the farmers' daughters and village girls were attracted to the handsome stranger and were, no doubt, available to lie with but, chastened by his recent tragic affair, he refrained from involvement. However, a frequent visitor at the farm was a quite young and very beautiful girl, daughter of the neighbouring farm owned by the Cooke family. (Johnny was not to know that his grandfather, John, had been more than friendly with another daughter.) Doris Cooke was, of course, interested in the young man from overseas and they became fast friends but not yet lovers.

Johnny entered Oxford without problems, explaining that it was considered advantageous for him to complete a degree at Oxford rather than at Harvard. He settled down to a quiet, studious period and in two years had achieved a good pass in History. During vacations, he travelled extensively around the British Isles but always visited the farm, and Doris Cooke, which he found was doing well, helped by his financial contribution and improved climatic conditions.

He came down from Oxford and spent some months on the farm, seeing much of London and making friends. It was 1853 and Johnny twenty years of age. Turkey had declared war on Russia, the latter seeking to expand its dominion into Europe and also was probing along the North West Frontier of India. The Turkish Navy was defeated, destroyed in the Black Sea by a superior Russian force. A joint Franco-British fleet moved into the Black Sea to protect the Turkish coast and block further movement by the Russians into the Mediterranean Sea. Johnny was quite convinced that war was imminent and decided to join the British army. He was, after all, of British descent.

Discussing his decision with the family, William Collins said that there was a retired general living in the village and would introduce Johnny to him to seek his advice. The general was quite impressed by the background of Johnny's forebears: a grandfather, major of the Hussars killed at Badajoz, his father a US cavalry captain, later lieutenant-colonel, who had lost an arm in the Indian Wars. The general said that Johnny's grandfather's regiment was currently serving in India but that his own regiment the 11th Hussars were in London, and that he would give him a letter of introduction. The 11th Hussars were a very prestigious regiment with a splendid record of achievements in action. They wore cherry-coloured trousers as a memento of an incident during the Peninsular War. Having been caught by French cavalry picking cherries in a large orchard, they successfully fought off the French and were henceforth known as the 'Cherry Pickers'.

The colonel of the 11th Hussars was agreeable that Johnny could purchase a commission in the regiment and sent him to the War Office for the formalities of induction, also where to obtain uniforms and accoutrements, all very costly but within his purse. In due course, Johnny presented himself to Knightsbridge Barracks near Hyde park. He was a very distinguished-looking young man, welcomed by the officers who were curious about his American background. He was posted to a troop under a senior lieutenant until ready to take over his own small command. With the likelihood of war against Russia, the army was training very hard. There were drills, manoeuvres and exercises day after day until the men achieved a peak of readiness.

The horses were the finest and the cavalrymen the best in the world. Nevertheless, generally the record of the cavalry on the field of battle was not impressive. The deficiency was in the officers who treated the act of war as a fox hunt: dash and ride over everything. The aristocratic generals were basically ignorant of the principles of war and served by incompetent staff officers, qualifications being rank, influence and privilege. This was particularly highlighted in the forthcoming war which was conducted by cavalry generals. The Duke of Wellington had remarked that the cavalry of other armies won battles but his had invariably got him in troublesome situations. The duke had died a year previously and the army was to miss his military genius.

In the spring of 1854, Britain and France declared war on Russia, together in support of the Ottoman Empire and against Russian expansionist ambitions in the Balkans. Russia's excuse was the necessity to protect the Orthodox Christians in the Ottoman Empire which extended into the Balkans. The Russians had already occupied the Turkish provinces of Moldavia and Walachia.

The army made ready to leave, although preparations were not very thorough. The high ranking officers were accepted to have received the cloak of Wellington but in detail and planning many important items were ignored. Lord Raglan was appointed commander-in-chief, Lord Lucan commanded the cavalry division, with Lord Cardigan leading the Light Brigade. Sailing ships were used instead of steamships which would have been better for the cavalry.

The latter were not immediately available but probably could have been found in time. Sailing ships required a round two months of the journey and steamers two to three weeks, which would have been better for the horses. Each regiment required five or six transports and the embarkation of the troop horses was carried out with much difficulty.

The holds of the sailing ships were small: confined space for horses and foul. Horses are bad sailors. There were many so sick that they could not stand. When one fell, others followed suit. There were frantic scenes of stamping, screaming horses, with the men trying to get them up and pacify them. The storms in the Bay of Biscay were terrible and the Mediterranean, although an inland sea, can be uncomfortably rough. The men were also sick and Johnny, who was not so afflicted, spent much of the time below.

'Not done, old boy,' he was told.

Because of his American upbringing, he considered that mucking in under the circumstances was desirable.

The Earl of Cardigan, the Light Brigade commander, did not suffer such handicaps. He travelled across France in great style, was entertained by the Emperor Napoleon III and continued by steamship from Marseilles, arriving at Scutari, the British base, at the end of May. When he reported to Lord Lucan, the divisional commander, he was met with displeasure. The two officers disliked each other intensely, which did not augur well for the future.

The scene at Varna, where the army were gathering prior to landing on the Crimea, at present not decided where, was a shambles. Stores and equipment were lying around in disorderly fashion. All that was clear was to take Sebastopol and deny the Russians access to the Black Sea. Lord Lucan was left behind at Scutari. Cardigan was seemingly in charge of the cavalry division and their dislike grew to the extent of the exchanging of acrimonious letters. The commander-in-chief, Lord Raglan, communicated with Cardigan, by-passing Lucan, which made matters worse. Seemingly only the fighting spirit and endurance of the common soldier remained. Lord Cardigan lived on a palatial yacht and only came ashore as necessary.

THE CRIMEA - THEATRE OF OPERATIONS

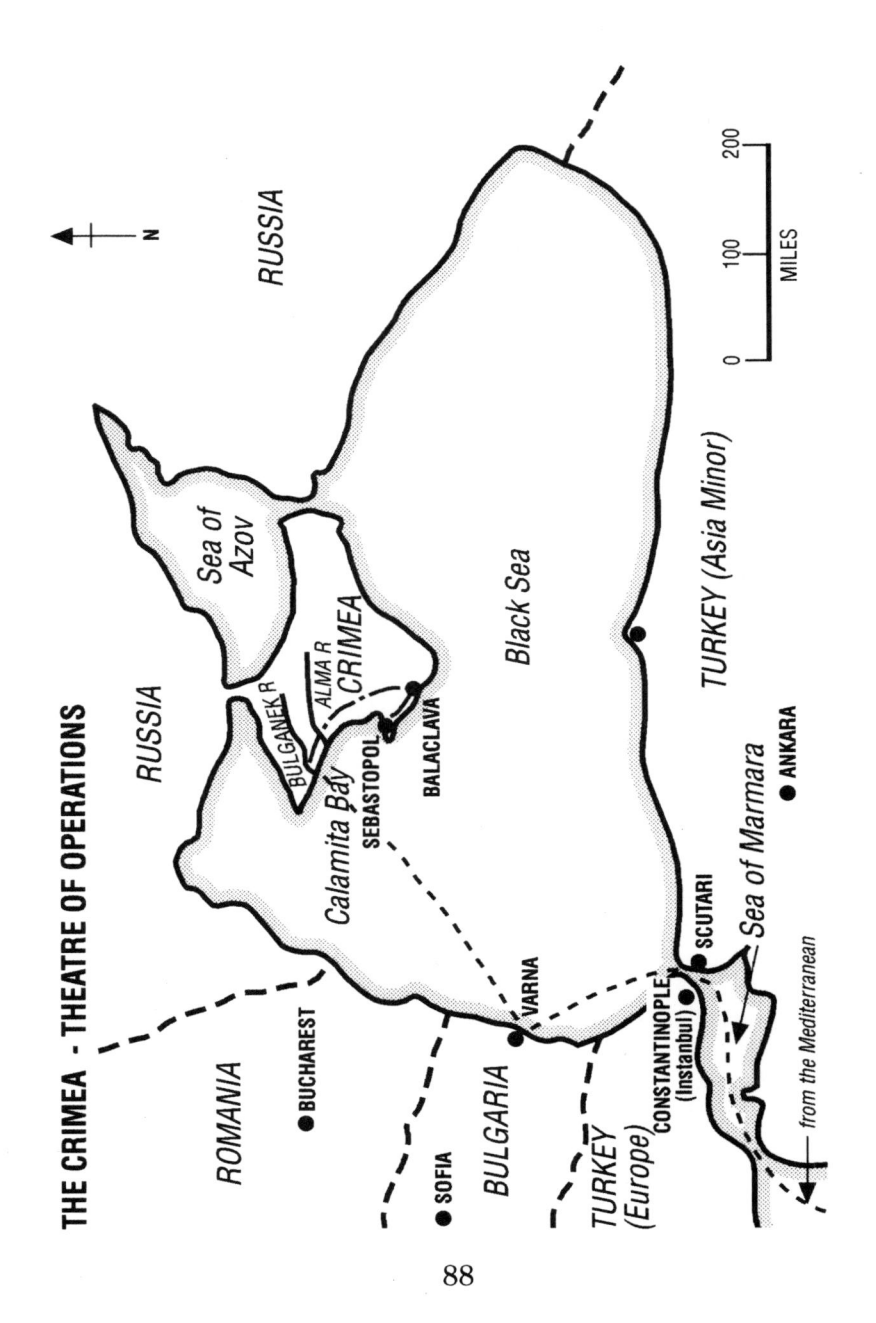

19

In June the Turks announced that they had driven the Russians out of Silistria, on the Danube River, and the latter had retreated across the river. Silistria was about a hundred miles from Varna, through Bulgaria in barren country to the north-west. In order to conform this, Lord Raglan ordered Lord Cardigan to send a patrol to ascertain the situation on the spot and to establish the whereabouts of the Russians. Cardigan decided to go himself and assembled a patrol, which was quite unnecessarily, a small fighting force of some two hundred men from the 8th Hussars and the 17th Lancers. Considering speed to be the object, Cardigan left with a minimum of food and forage, at a cracking pace. On arrival, they did find that the Russians had gone but did not locate them, although the enemy was indeed watching the British patrolling up and down.

On the return journey the patrol suffered from heat exhaustion, overwork and lack of forage and water, a situation considered by the army to be unnecessary suffering. Some horses dropped dead. A hundred were dying, a serious loss, and the remainder were mostly unfit for anything but light work. Vital information regarding the whereabouts of the enemy had not been established. It was, all in all, a total waste. Lord Raglan was justifiably angry, particularly at the loss of valuable horses. He bypassed Lucan, who was still at Scutari, and Cardigan, and ordered the 11th Hussars to send a patrol, not a small army, and definitely to locate the enemy.

The major commanding the 11th, the colonel being sick, decided to send Johnny, whom he had remarked on the ship had a good rapport with his men, and handled the horses well. He left the details to Johnny, who firstly spoke with an officer of the 8th to gain information about the route. Johnny selected his sergeant and six troopers and sufficient baggage horses and with reasonable speed, not exerting the horses, duly arrived at Silistria. There was no sign of the Russians so he decided to take his sergeant across the Danube by night. At daylight, a careful reconnaissance revealed that the enemy were there and he spent the day observing their dispositions and strength. Recrossing at night, they set out at once for Varna. The success of the patrol, at no loss of horses or men, was applauded and the valuable information they brought was well-received by Lord Raglan who commended the 11th and the officer who led the patrol.

The army was now ready to embark to land on the Crimea, at a suitable area that had been reconnoitred in the Bay of Calamita. To Lord Cardigan's chagrin, Lord Lucan arrived to take over the division and a great row broke out which was finally quashed by Lord Raglan's ruling that Lucan was the divisional commander and Cardigan commander of the Light Brigade. To establish his position, Lord Lucan was promoted from major general to lieutenant general.

The embarkation was a scene of confusion. Lack of space caused much hardship. Men were so tightly packed that they could barely turn round. It was necessary to leave behind much of the stores and equipment, to the detriment of future operations and causing more hardship. The soldiers' wives were forbidden to go to the Crimea but at the last moment a mob of screaming women invaded the ships and had to be crammed in.

The army were glad to leave Bulgaria where cholera had raged. Many were dead and flung into the sea. Unfortunately, the cholera sailed with them and was to severely diminish the strength of the army. The fleet of some five hundred ships rendezvoused with the French at the mouth of the Danube and inexplicably remained there for several days, with increased discomfort and more bodies being thrown into the sea. The delay was caused, it transpired, because although the place in the Crimea was agreed, those who were in charge of the operation had not been informed. To add to this unhappy situation, Cardigan was made up to major general and felt once more secure in exchanging acrimonious letters with Lucan.

Finally, the fleet got going and sailed into Calamita Bay and the following morning disembarkation commenced, fortunately, to everyone's surprise, unopposed, although the Russians were known to be in strength not so far away. The army, when landed, was in a sorry state, suffering from diarrhoea and dysentery, in addition to cholera. Matters were made worse by lack of tents and medical supplies being left at Varna, and many died. Lord Raglan decided that it would be worse to wait and the British and French, sixty thousand strong, began to march across barren empty and waterless land suffering from thirst as there was no way of replenishing their canteens, a situation not remedied until they reached the Bulganek River.

From the Bulganek, a recce was ordered towards Alma and Johnny's squadron was to do this, led by the major who was still commanding the 11th. They moved with great caution, as they could expect to encounter Cossack cavalry patrols which, indeed, they did. But, warned by their scouts ahead of the squadron, they were not detected. As they approached within sight of the Alma, they found themselves on a flat grassy plain with high precipitous ground across the river and could detect the Russians there on the escarpment. It was impossible for the squadron to go further so the major, recalling Johnny's exploit at Silistria on the Danube, decided to send him over the Alma, suggesting that he take the same men with him. He was to proceed on foot at dusk, allowing himself only two days to carry out the task, as the British were on the move and it was very urgent to have the information. Of course, Johnny was understandably equipped to carry out the work due to his education. Generally cavalry officers did not bother with formal learning, usually being only interested in riding, hunting and shooting and a good time.

They crossed the river, which had a steep bank on the other side, and then there was an uphill climb to the parapet-like escarpment. They managed to get to the top with some difficulty, appreciating the problem of getting troops up and seeking the best approaches. They lay up in concealment observing the Russians for a whole day, Johnny making notes and sketches, and returning at night to arrive back at the squadron by first light. The major was very pleased and, uncaring about being discovered, pressed on back to the approaching Allies. The report emphasized that the attack would have to be carried out against withering fire from artillery and small arms.

The army advanced until within range where details could be seen with the naked eye and the battle commenced with an attack by the French, on the right towards the sea, aided by the guns of the Fleet.

20

Before reaching the Alma, Lord Raglan sent a staff officer to the 11th. He wished to speak with the officer who had made the recce to obtain further information. Johnny accompanied the staff officer and replied competently to the general's questions. The general, realizing that he was not a native Englishman, enquired of his ancestry and was quite impressed by his background, his Hussar grandfather, his US cavalry father, his education at both Harvard and Oxford.

On his return, Johnny found that the infantry had crossed the river and were struggling up the slopes, enduring furious cannonade from the Russian guns on the heights. The cavalry were not engaged. It certainly was not for mounted troops. However, a regiment of Cossacks was seen to be approaching along the north bank and the 11th were ordered to attack them. The Hussars moved out in extended order of two lines, one squadron in reserve. They hit the Cossacks at the charge, catching them undecided and wrong-footed. It was rather one-sided. The Russians immediately suffered serious casualties and hastily broke away. It was Johnny's first taste of blood and he acquitted himself well and found it all very exhilarating.

The ferocious courage and tenacity of the British troops carried the day, in spite of the ineptness of the generals on both sides. The French had succeeded in gaining a foothold on the lower heights towards the sea. The Russian general panicked and the British advanced stubbornly up the deadly glacier, raked by musket fire and cannon, led by the Light Infantry division of Peninsula fame. Their blood was up, even if only a few got there they were determined to reach the Russian redoubt and so they did. The opposition was now much reduced and the Light Division was quickly reinforced by others but they also came under heavy fire from another standpoint. The Guards, the Highlanders, and Fusiliers had many casualties and the British dead piled up on the slope.

The French artillery had now been brought up and was in action, causing great damage to the enemy. The Russian guns silenced, the British infantry now faced a vast number of enemy infantry advancing across the escarpment. The British horse artillery crossed the river and were able to give support from a flank position. Slowly, the enemy gave way before the determined assault and the Highlanders broke through and the Russians finally gave up, turned and ran. The cavalry moved up to the heights and pursued the fleeing hordes, inflicting great damage. Lord Raglan called off the pursuit, not wishing to risk the precious cavalry and so, reluctantly, they broke off the chase.

At the end of September the Allies began advancing southwards, closely watched by circling Cossacks. It was very hot and again there was little water. The troops were heavily burdened and suffered terribly.

In a week of hard marching the Allies reached Balaclava, south of the ultimate goal, Sebastopol. Balaclava, a port, was suited as a base for the British where the fleet could supply them and already ships were arriving, having been following the advance. An attack on Sebastopol was feasible but Raglan would not accept the risk. Other commanders were furious, feeling that a valuable opportunity had been lost. The Russians were also gathering in force on the plains approaching Balaclava and no attempt was made by the cavalry division to harass them. They were held back by the generals, much to the chagrin of the troopers who were raring to go.

Lord Cardigan's yacht also arrived in the harbour and there he spent his nights in luxury whilst the soldiers endured the hardships of salt pork in the open because the

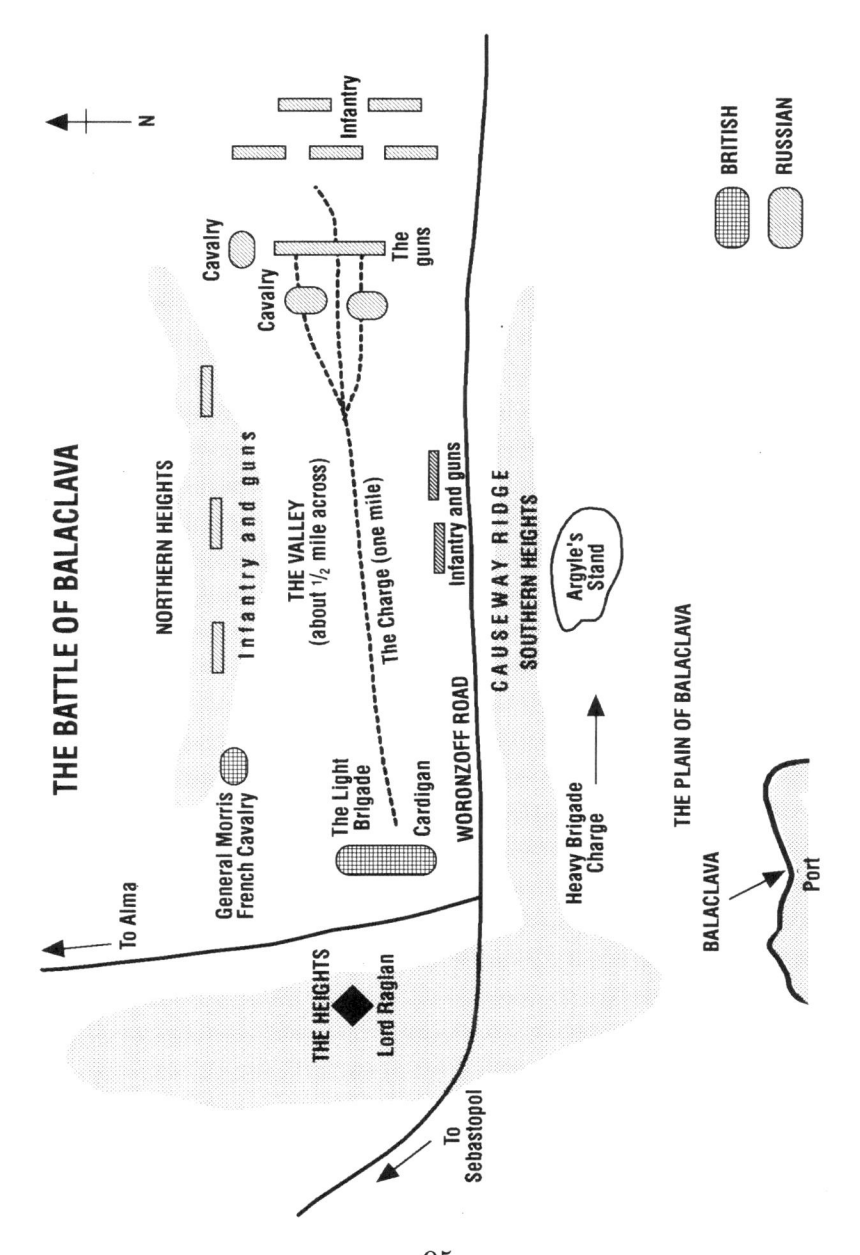

THE BATTLE OF BALACLAVA

NORTHERN HEIGHTS

Infantry

Infantry and guns

Cavalry

Cavalry

The guns

THE VALLEY (about 1/2 mile across)

The Charge (one mile)

Infantry and guns

WORONZOFF ROAD

CAUSEWAY RIDGE

SOUTHERN HEIGHTS

Argyle's Stand

General Morris French Cavalry

The Light Brigade

Cardigan

Heavy Brigade Charge

THE PLAIN OF BALACLAVA

To Alma

THE HEIGHTS
Lord Raglan

To Sebastopol

BALACLAVA

Port

N

BRITISH
RUSSIAN

95

bivouacs had still not arrived. Siege guns were landed and established round Sebastopol and the fortress was heavily shelled and there was a great explosion when the magazine blew up. Still no attack was mounted as the British and French could not agree on a plan. This hesitation was to prove costly and another year passed before the end of the Crimean War and peace with Russia.

Sickness was still rampant. Cholera and dysentery ravaged the army, many officers were casualties and at regimental level numbers were inadequate. Not entirely due to this shortage but on overall merit, Johnny was promoted, without purchase, to the rank of captain which meant that he would certainly be commanding a squadron or even the regiment.

Due to the massive build-up of the enemy forces to the east of Balaclava it was all too apparent that an attack would come from there. Reinforcements were streaming in and before the end of October the Allies assessed that they were confronted by more than twenty-five battalions of infantry and a similar amount of cavalry with many guns. In effect, the British were enclosed in Balaclava, their only supply route, and with no other line of communication. Lord Raglan was short of men and had reluctantly placed the cavalry in front: the Light Brigade in the valley and the Heavy Brigade on the Balaclava Plain. Perhaps casualties would have been less at Alma, apart from sickness, if the generals had recalled the Duke of Wellington's successful attacks at night. Lord Raglan also completely ignored the Turks as bandits and only used them inside Balaclava: an error of judgement because they had fought well at Silistria.

A Turkish spy brought information that several divisions of infantry and cavalry were approaching towards Balaclava to the south-east below the Causeway. Previous intelligence had been ignored and not investigated. However, the army was stood to in the bitter cold and many died from exposure, including the commanding officer of the 17th Lancers.

The following morning, at daybreak, a great enemy force

was seen advancing along the causeway towards Balaclava and all that was in their way was the Heavy Brigade and the Argyle Highlanders. The Heavy Brigade with its Horse Artillery put on a brave show but did not actually engage, eventually withdrawing towards Balaclava and the end of the causeway. Lord Cardigan now arrived from his yacht, half-asleep still. Lord Raglan ordered infantry divisions to move down from the heights and the cavalry were to await their arrival.

The Russians still came on, meeting the Argyles who stood firm so that the enemy had no idea what they were facing and halted. A great profusion of conflicting and confusing orders came down from the Heights, having no effect whatsoever on the situation below. Wellington would have turned over in his grave. A body of some four thousand Russian cavalry were posed above on the Causeway Heights and facing the Heavy Brigade, about five hundred strong. The Heavy Brigade was composed of very illustrious regiments: the Scots, Greys, Royals, Enniskillen, 4th and 5th Dragoon guards, all perfectly trained and superbly disciplined.

The Russian cavalry commenced to move down and the Heavy Brigade rode headlong up the slope, crashing into the Russian mass seemingly engulfed but in fact fighting like maniacs, hacking and slashing. Unbelievably, the enemy mass broke and fled away uphill, finally rushing away over the causeway to the north. The brilliant victory was not followed up. The Russians got away and the Light Brigade, ordered to stand fast although begging to be let loose, were furious at the lost opportunity to follow the advantage. As it happened, the Russians got away and firmly established themselves at the eastern end of the valley. The splendid achievement of the Heavy Brigade was wasted, except that it did halt the threat to Balaclava. The Light Brigade was ordered to take up position at the entrance to the north valley with the Heavy Brigade behind them on the slopes of the causeway, and to await the arrival of two divisions of infantry which were now moving down from the heights. By

Lord Raglan's previous holding back of the cavalry, Lord Lucan clearly understood that the cavalry were not to attack alone. In spite of this, a terrible error in message writing was to cause the opposite to take place. The enemy still held redoubts on the Causeway Heights, on the hills above the north valley and the end of the valley a mile away. The Valley itself was empty.

Then came the order from Raglan to Lucan which resulted in the Charge of the Light Brigade. The message ordered the cavalry to advance to the front to prevent the enemy from carrying away the guns. The guns referred to were British cannon left behind on the Causeway Heights which Raglan, from the Heights, could see, the Russians having removed captured guns to indicate a victory.

Lucan could not see this from below and said to the staff officer, 'What guns?'

The officer replied, pointing down the valley, 'There are your guns,' indicating the Russian artillery a mile away. The officer also repeated Raglan's last words to him as he left with the written orders, 'Tell Lord Lucan that the cavalry is to attack immediately.'

Lord Lucan thought that the order for cavalry to attack artillery was absurd but, nevertheless, ordered Lord Cardigan to advance on the guns at the end of the valley. The Brigade was drawn up in three lines: in front the 13th Light Dragoons and the 17th Lancers, the latter commanded by Captain Morris, he who had begged Lucan to follow up the Charge of the Heavy Brigade; the second the 11th Hussars, with Johnny leading a squadron; the third line, the 4th Light Dragoons and the 8th Hussars, perfectly dressed Lord Cardigan leading from the front quite alone. Some of the regiments were led by captains, senior commanders being dead or sick.

Lord Cardigan gave the order, 'The Brigade will advance, walk, trot,' and they moved off as if on a parade ground review, perfectly dressed.

The Light Brigade advanced with superb precision, Lord

Cardigan riding out there alone, in spite of his faults, a very gallant figure, showing great courage, splendid in the uniform of the 11th Hussars, his old regiment. Shortly after moving, the Russian guns opened up together with the riflemen on the Causeway Heights and the hills to the north, catching the brigade in a deadly crossfire. Still the small force trotted on with absolute precision, closing ranks when horses fell. Soon they were in reach of the guns at the end of the valley and round shot and grape mowed men down.

The French General observed, '*C'est magnifique, mai ce n'est pas la guerre.*'

The Heavy Brigade, following, met with the same intense fire, suffering also many casualties. Lord Lucan, seeing the destruction of the Light Brigade, with unusual common sense ordered them to retreat, not wishing to lose the whole brigade. The French colonial cavalry, commanded by General Morris, appreciating the horrific plight of the Light Brigade, advanced across the northern hills, charging and causing the Russian artillery and infantry to retreat resulting in a brilliant success.

Meanwhile, down below the inferno of fire went on, with many troopers crashing to the ground and Lord Cardigan still maintaining the steady trot until, after some minutes had passed and the ranks ever closing up, he broke into a gallop, followed by what was left of the front rank. Close to the Russian guns, a salvo practically destroyed the first line but with the few survivors, Lord Cardigan, miraculously unhurt, galloped furiously into the cursed guns, closely followed by what was left of the Brigade. In the battery there was furious fighting and slaughter. The Russian gunners, trying unsuccessfully to extricate themselves and the guns, struggled in a dense pall of smoke.

The remaining Light Brigade survivors passed suddenly out of the smoke and found themselves confronted by a great cloud of Russian Cavalry waiting behind the guns.

Captain Morris, with those left of the 17th Lancers, and Johnny, of the 11th Hussars, unable to stop, crashed into the enemy who, taken completely by surprise, did nothing except fire a few pistol shots. The British recovered and turned back into the guns. Captain Morris saw Johnny reeling in the saddle, rode alongside him and, stirrup to stirrup, supported him. And so they eventually returned back.

The way back was not so bad. The fire from the Northern Hills had been stopped by General Morris and his Chasseurs, that from the head of the Valley had ceased and only the causeway guns were active. The way was made horrific by the dead, dying and wounded men and horses. Lord Cardigan was the first one out of the guns and arrived at the division before the others. This gave rise to the rumour that he had not gone into the Russian guns nor through them, a belief which was unconfirmed. Others did witness that he had gone through but were not very convincing.

So, the wrong guns and an incomplete message. The guns intended to be attacked were those on the Woronzoff Road, the causeway slopes. The aide-de-camp who brought the message and pointed out the guns at the head of the valley, rode with the charge and, realizing his mistake, pressed to the front to warn Lord Cardigan but was killed by a shell, too late.

Record has it that six hundred and seventy-three attacked, one hundred and thirteen were killed and one hundred and thirty-four wounded, all in a very short time. Alfred Lord Tennyson wrote a magnificent poem, *The Charge of the Light Brigade*, containing the famous lines:

> Their's not to reason why,
> Their's but to do and die;
> Into the Valley of Death
> Rode the six hundred.

The Russians locked themselves up in Sebastopol. There was a battle at Inkerman where the British Infantry roundly defeated them and Sebastopol was under siege for one year, until September 1855.

Perhaps, apart from the glorious cavalry charge, the only noteworthy things to emerge from the Crimea were articles of clothing: the cardigan, the raglan overcoat and the balaclava helmet. There was also a very important event – the beginning of organized hospital nursing and, possibly, the Red Cross society.

21

Johnny was sorely wounded, his right leg pierced, tibia and fibia bones fractured and the muscle torn away at the exit of the ball and, in addition, another ball had passed along his left ribs, gouging a great furrow. After cleaning up, bandaging and splinting and the leg being very fortunately well set by the surgeon, he was put on hospital transport and delivered to the military hospital at Scutari.

The hospital was appalling, dirty and disorganized and men were dying from lack of care, a situation which Florence Nightingale, a trained nurse, with a group of ladies sent out by the government, was making a strenuous effort to remedy. She was accustomed to make nightly rounds carrying a lantern and consequently was named, 'The Lady of the Lamp'. Her efforts made a great improvement in the conditions under which the wounded and sick were kept. She instituted army nursing and later on return to England set up a training school for nurses at St Thomas's Hospital in London.

Johnny was given a curtained off corner of a ward which he shared with another wounded officer of the 8th Hussars. His ribs responded to daily dressings by a lady nurse and his leg was redressed and splinted by a surgeon who said that all seemed well and that recovery would be in a short few weeks unless the wound became infected. The nurse was a very lively young woman and Johnny obviously became interested, so much so that he became erect when she was doing his dressings and bathing him.

She was well aware of his arousal and one day said, 'I am sure that I can help you with your problem. I will come tonight after Miss Nightingale's rounds.'

Well, she came with another young woman to take care of the 8th Hussar. After preliminary embracing, she climbed astride Johnny, that being the only way, as he must lie on his back. From the murmuring across the room obviously the others were doing likewise. Sex in company is extremely erotic and Johnny and the girl reached several shattering climaxes until exhausted and, in any case, it was getting light. Johnny was exhilarated. It did him the power of good and was repeated quite often, the young couple being very fond of each other and enjoying the sexual pleasures equally.

Johnny's recovery was quite remarkable, due not least to the special therapy he was receiving, and in a few weeks he could get around on crutches. The surgeon considered that he was fit to travel and could leave on the next transport for England. The journey was without incident and even the Bay of Biscay was calm. On arrival he was sent for a check-up at a military hospital in London and pronounced fit to convalesce at home. James Collins visited him with his son William and arranged to take him to The Farm, where a hero's welcome awaited.

Practically the whole village turned out to welcome Johnny Collins. After all, there were few who had actually taken part in the legendary Charge of the Light Brigade, an event which was forever to stir the hearts of many, particularly schoolboys.

Johnny was anxious to see Doris Cooke. Was she still free and would she remember him? he wondered. Of course, she called at The Farm at the first opportunity, which was almost immediately on his arrival, and there was no doubt about her joy. At the first opportunity Johnny proposed marriage to her which, of course, she accepted and the families were delighted. They were married in the parish church, a splendid wedding, the guard of honour being provided by Johnny's brother officers, the 11th having returned to England. A honeymoon was spent in London at the best hotel, Johnny was now able to walk comfortably using a walking cane.

Soon Johnny reported back to the regiment for duty as he did not want to leave the army and to his pleasure was appointed as adjutant of the depot, the regimental home. He was able to live most nights at The Farm, his duties being light but quite interesting.

After a year, Doris bore him a daughter and later a son who was christened James, after the current relative who although of old age still carried on aided by his son William who was of early middle age, married and having several children.

Towards the end of the decade, rumblings were coming out of America, the South against the North, the abolitionists pressing for the end of slavery in the South being the principal cause of the dissension. In addition, the Southern States objected to federal control over them, insisting on states' rights. Compromise failed and conflict loomed. Johnny was anxious about the situation and thought that they should visit his parents, to which Doris agreed.

As a first step he purchased a majority, very costly but he could afford it. He then applied for a leave of absence of one year on half-pay on the grounds that the worsening situation in America necessitated a visit to his parents' home there. He was granted leave and advised, in view of the circumstances in America and the likelihood of a Civil War breaking out, to keep in close touch as his services might well be required there.

Johnny lost no time. They packed for a long stay in America and took the train to Liverpool where he had booked passage on a steamer to New York. Compared with the sailing ships, it provided a much shorter and more comfortable journey. From New York, where they spent a few days, they travelled on to the South by the various railways, eventually arriving at Columbia and on to Ridgeway and The Oaks plantation.

Part Four

America

1857–1862

SKETCH MAP OF US AMERICA

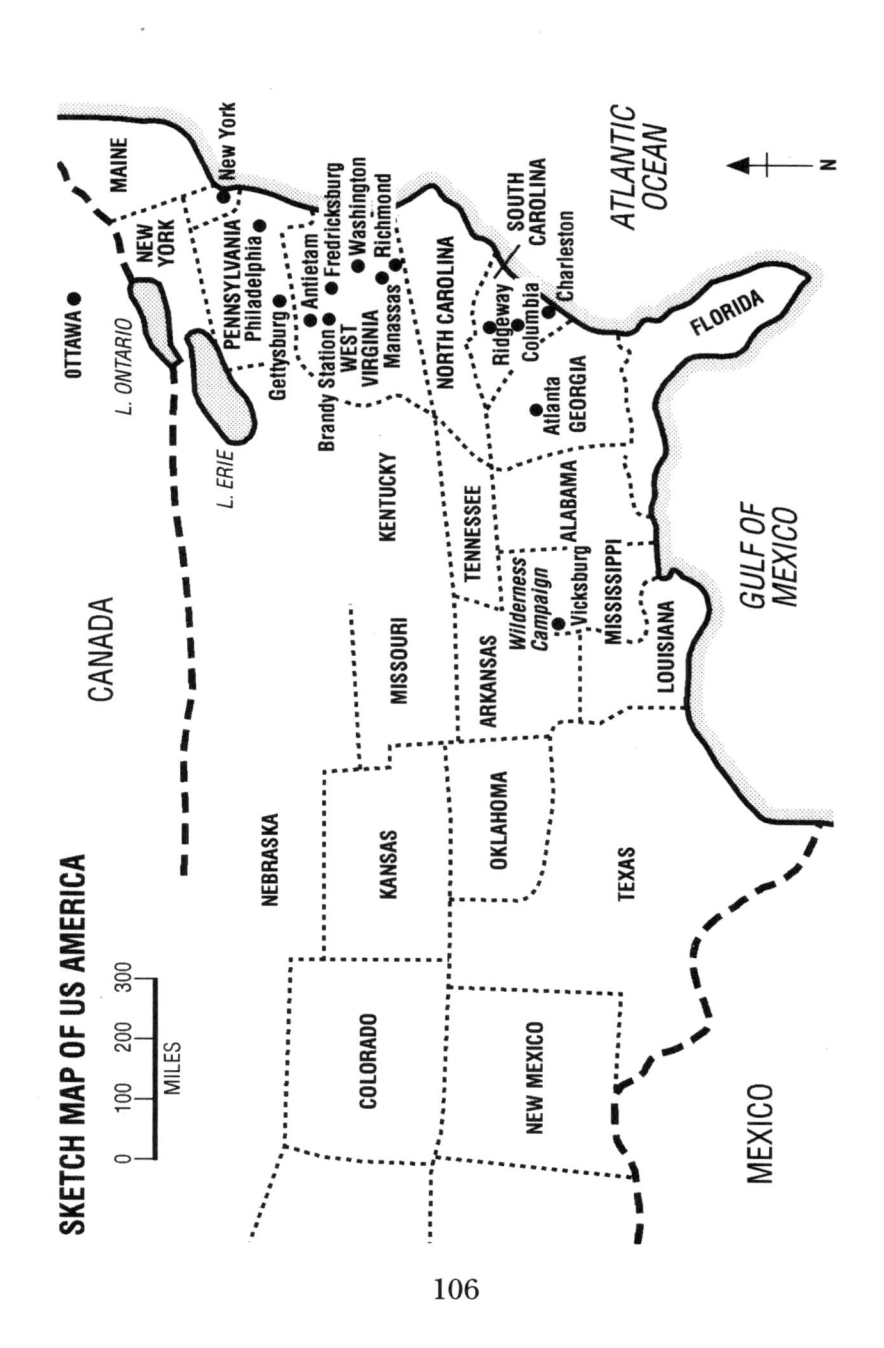

22

They were welcomed rapturously by Johnny's parents, Juan and Mary, and the now somewhat aged grandparents. They were particularly proud of Johnny's exploits in the Crimean War, delighted with the children, regaling them with parties to meet the county people.

It was early 1861, Abraham Lincoln was president, very opposed to slavery and determined to maintain state control of the South by the federal government. A worsening situation caused the Southern States into a secession under a confederation led by Jefferson Davis.

In April, General Beauregard ordered Confederates to fire on Fort Sumter, so hostilities began. Johnny at once contacted the War Office in London and was instructed to present himself to Jefferson Davis with a letter of introduction as an observing officer. The War Office also instructed him to note carefully and report on the handling of the conflict by the generals, conduct of the troops, the arms and supply arrangements. He was passed on to Beauregard who received him with curiosity, asking about his background, his regiment and his experiences of the Crimea and was quite impressed.

The general sent him to JEB Stuart saying, 'You will see everything with him.'

James Ewell Brown Stuart was then twenty-eight years of age, commander of the Confederate Cavalry, probably the most brilliant cavalry commander of all time. He excelled in gathering information about the enemy, location, strength, movement and arms, was an excellent raider and marauder intercepting enemy supplies; no frontal attacks against guns and infantry, only when supported by the infantry and artillery. JEB was known as the Flower of Cavaliers. He was flamboyant, with ostrich plumed hat and scarlet-lined cloak and his splendid horse, Skylark.

Johnny presented himself to Stuart who was very interested in his story, particularly of the famous Charge, echoing Maréchal Bosquet's comment that it was splendid but hardly war. He told Johnny to stay close with his staff, not to engage in the fighting except to defend himself.

'You are going to see some vicious fighting', he said, 'and we cannot afford to lose our way of life. We are not like the cold, dour, preaching Northerners.'

The Confederates had advanced to Manassas, not far from Washington, when Stuart's cavalry reported a strong Union force proceeding rapidly towards them. Beauregard disposed his forces, covering the woods and meadows from where the blue coats would appear, placing Thomas Jackson's Virginia Brigade in the centre. Meanwhile, Johnny riding with the cavalry noted how skilfully JEB directed the shadowing of the Dowell's Union army and at the same time picking off any who straggled away from the main body. Civilians came out from Washington on horseback and family carriages to see the fun and were alarmed to encounter Confederate grey clad horsemen, and some fleeing back along the road to Washington.

Blue coats appeared coming out of the woods in force and Stuart's cavalry lured them on to Thomas Jackson's Brigade. So began the short-lived Battle of Manassas, also known as Bull Run. The Union force was met by a hail of rifle and cannon fire but attacked repeatedly, without success, Jackson held 'like a stonewall' and was henceforth known at Stonewall Jackson, next to R.E. Lee, the most celebrated general of the Confederates. McDowell, retreating in a rout, was pursued by Stuart to the gates of Washington. First blood to the rebels. Johnny had been allowed to go with the forward skirmishes and had sight of the Capitol at Washington, the soldiers and civilians being sucked back into the city.

The second Battle of Bull Run, or Manassas, took place in the summer of 1862 when the Yankees under General McClellan were trying to reinforce the army along the Rappahannock River which divided the two armies. Stonewall Jackson under the commander-in-chief of the Confederates, General Robert E. Lee, again stopped them and it was back into Washington. The cavalry, seizing the opportunity, chased the Union blue-coats picking up stragglers and collecting booty discarded on the way. Johnny had his second view of the city.*

In the spring and early summer of 1862, General McClellan set the Union Forces in motion from Washington in an attempt to take the Confederates' capital city, Richmond, Virginia. Known as the Peninsular Campaign, the action was generally on the Peninsula between York and James rivers. The outcome was achieved by a brilliant action by Stonewall Jackson in the Shenandoah Valley and the Southern victory resulted in the retreat of the Yankees to Washington.

JEB Stuart maintained close watch on Washington and at once reported the movement of McClellan. Johnny was accompanying a squadron strength patrol, closely observing the blue-coats when, unfortunately emerging from a sunken road, they found themselves surrounded by enemy infantry. Their point scouts had been silently disposed of, so without any warning of the danger they were obliged to surrender. Johnny, in his strange 11th Hussars uniform, was subject to considerable interest. He explained to the officer in charge of the unit that he was a non-combatant, British officer accredited to the Confederate Army as an observer, as were others situated with the Union Army. He was sent back to the colonel of the regiment who was somewhat amused and dined Johnny well, impressed by his involvement in the Crimea and, of course, the famous charge at Balaclava. Johnny's father's service with the US Cavalry in the Indian

* The Third Battle of Manassas took place very recently when it was proposed to construct a theme park on the site of the battle, the theme being the Civil War. The proposers lost.

Wars also gained the captive considerable regard.

Finally, Johnny was sent back to McClellan's headquarters and eventually reached the general himself who, like the former colonel, was quite impressed by Johnny's story. Questions about the Confederates were ignored and the general respected the neutrality of an observing officer. The general decided to send his prize captive back to Washington and recommended that he be handed over to the British ambassador.

Suitably escorted and after much further questioning by the War Department, he was delivered to the ambassador, a peer of the realm. The ambassador was delighted to receive Johnny. He himself was a military man and had seen service with the cavalry and he insisted that Johnny stay at this residence. Briefly it was decided that Johnny could further his mission by gaining information about the Union Army whilst obliged to remain there and to that end he would contact one of the observing officers. What to do with Johnny later, he would consider. Johnny explained that his parents, wife and children were in the South and, of course, he was anxious to see them. The ambassador said that he would get news to them anyway. Meanwhile, he would also contact the War Office in London. Johnny was duly installed in the residence, being introduced to the lady ambassadress, who was younger than the ambassador and very attractive. She made him very welcome and said that she looked forward to hearing of his adventures. With an impulsive insight she told the butler to put Johnny in rooms away from the principal bedrooms, to provide him with peace and quiet.

That night the ambassador gave a dinner party to which important people were invited. They were intrigued by the strange officer's appearance on the scene and quite enthralled by his story, particularly of the Charge of the Light Brigade. The lady ambassadress indicated by covert overtures her interest in the vigorous, comparatively young man who was not unaware of the possible invitation to a closer relationship.

Johnny retired when the party was finally over very late and went to bed, leaving his candles alight, thinking of her. Sure enough, silently the door opened and there she was, clad in a long white robe which when discarded revealed her body quite naked and very lovely, except for very elegant riding boots.

'Young man I am going to ride you as you rode your horse at Balaclava,' she said.

Johnny stood out like a tent pole and she climbed astride, engulfing him in her warm wet cavern.

She began a rhythmic motion, walk, trot, faster-canter, gallop until 'Aaah Ooooh,' she cried, reaching a multiple orgasm, 'I am coming all the time, I can't stop coming,' 'Oooh,' she moaned and collapsed, half-conscious, on to Johnny. He was so astonished that he did not finish with her, so kept on steadily thrusting upwards until it was over and she, in the last throes climaxed again.

They were to repeat this often during Johnny's stay but never again with such intensity. She declared herself to be truly in love with him, in spite of the knowledge that their affair had no future. He also was very fond of her and said that she was the best lover he had ever had or was likely to encounter in the future. Both were very grateful to each other. Of course, all was kept very secret and they behaved very circumspectly when with others. The old ambassador, long since without sex, slept alone, quite unaware of the goings-on.

As arranged by the ambassador, an observing officer, a British lieutenant colonel of the Guards appointed to the Union Army met with Johnny and much useful information was exchanged. Together they compiled comparative lists of the two forces, strengths, arms, fighting ability, generalship etc., a very comprehensive report. It was decided to hold this until a reply was received from the War Office to the ambassador's letter informing them of Johnny's presence in Washington.

The days were spent very pleasantly and the nights even

more so. The lady did not wear riding boots again but suggested that she might well do so, perhaps with spurs. Such lovemaking neither would ever forget.

The reply from England ordered Johnny to return there and report to the War Office in person, prepared to provide all the information needed, particularly on weapons and ammunition, as the Americans had probably produced some new and improved armaments.

The ambassador arranged a passage on a steamer out of New York to Liverpool, now a very much quicker journey than by the old sailing ships. A friend of the ambassador, a wealthy businessman, requested Johnny to look after his daughter who was also booked on the ship, going to school in England, and she could travel with him to New York. Sincere farewells were made to the ambassador and more than just goodbye and a handshake for his darling wife. The young lady turned out to be a shy very pretty girl with a not unnoticeable figure. Johnny thought immediately, 'Here we go again.'

Part Five

England

1862

23

Johnny and Anne, for such was the young lady's name, boarded the train to New York with a tremendous send-off, impressing the other passengers. Johnny was in civilian dress but obviously a military man. Without incident, they arrived at New York, the city bustling with life, and took a carriage to the ship on the Hudson River. Johnny saw Anne to her cabin and thought to himself that he expected to be seeing inside before long. They arranged to meet for dinner in the lounge where there was a bar. Anne said that she liked wine, which she was accustomed to drink at home. After dinner they walked on the part of the deck reserved for passengers. The ship was now bearing away from the coast. The sea was calm and silvery under an almost full moon and as the night became cool they went down below to the cabin deck.

At Anne's cabin she practically dragged the not reluctant Johnny inside and firmly closed the door, clinging to him and kissing him fervently, to which of course, he responded.

She said, rather unnaturally, 'I love you, I am yours, please take me.'

Well, he thought this is it, feeling under her clothes. His fingers finding the place where, as he expected, it was firmly closed by her maidenhead.

'It is impossible. I cannot take you, it would not be right,' he said, 'but I will give you pleasure with my hand.'

Anne had two brothers and was not inexperienced. She uncovered his erect member and asked for his handkerchief.

They achieved satisfaction together and she said, 'But I still want you to break me.'

Johnny told her, 'We shall see. You are too young to be

injured. Better you wait until you are married.'

'We shall see,' she replied.

Satisfaction was effected but Anne was so insistent that the night before they arrived in Liverpool he gave up and with considerable force penetrated through the tough membrane and burrowed fully into her welcoming orifice and together they reached a happy conclusion. Anne was bleeding somewhat and exclaimed that she would never be able to walk again. Of course, on the morrow she was fit, well and very pleased.

They went ashore together and he escorted Anne to her waiting relatives, bidding her a formal farewell, the loving goodbye already having been said. Johnny took the train to London, vowing not to misbehave in future; to be chaste until he returned to the plantation in America.

24

Johnny travelled to London and went at once to Hampstead and the Farm where William Collins, now firmly in charge, welcomed him with delight and the whole family were overjoyed to have with them their hero. He recounted his adventures in the Civil War and eventual stay in New York. The Farm was now prospering. England was far from war and the industrial revolution was in full swing. William said that since Johnny had helped them with money in the lean time he considered the former a shareholder and there was a fair sum of money due to him.

Johnny thought for a while and said, 'I do not want for cash. Perhaps we can together set up a small charity to help the poor and sick in the parish.' William agreed to do this.

After resting a day he went to town, first to the Foreign Office to deliver letters from New York with the ambassador's personal communications, one regarding Johnny and his stay at the embassy. He then presented himself to the War Office where at the entrance the orderly referring to a list directed him to a staff colonel. The colonel said that he had been expecting Major Collins and welcomed him back. The officer explained that he would firstly discuss with Johnny general details of his observations and the combined report, including the observing officer with the Union Army whom he knew Johnny had met in New York. Afterwards Johnny would prepare a full report which the colonel, tapping a file on his desk, said that, with his Oxford learning in history, he was sure would be very thorough. Johnny was told to report back in two weeks when he would meet the general in charge of the department. Meanwhile, the colonel invited Johnny to briefly run through his observations.

Starting from the top, Johnny observed that the Confederate generalship was better than that of the North, General R.E. Lee displayed great ability in planning and, above all, in the assessment of the enemy's strength and probable moves. He was well-loved and respected by his officers and men. He was also not too bothered about the advantage the North had in supplies, arms and munitions. The generals in the North were far from permanent. As was customary, they were sacked and replaced after a defeat and so far had achieved no victories.

The troops were numerically equal as near as the inaccurate rosters showed, around seventy thousand on each side. The Confederates were all volunteers but the North was obliged to institute conscription. In both armies soldiers begged to go home for the harvests and perforce this was often allowed. In both armies the soldiers fought with great vigour and courage, incredibly steadfast in close order at the advance. The South had the advantage of a cause: independence and to preserve slavery. The Confederates were all white and absorbed most of the available able-bodied men. Towards the end of the first campaigns the South also introduced a form of conscription, not with great success because the manpower required was just not there.

The Union Cavalry regiments were very well armed with Sharps breech-loading carbines and the new Colt revolvers but they were less numerous and lacked the spirit, élan, verve, skill and dash of Stuart's considerable force, in spite of the latter's mediocre equipment. Johnny had brought home with him the latest Sharps Carbine and a Colt revolver which he gave to the colonel, saying that for the present there was nothing new with the Confederates.

The artillery in use was the same on both sides and in equal quantities. The principal gun was the twelve-pounder, firing solid shot at a maximum range of just under one mile and effectively at about one thousand yards. It also fired explosive shells and canister, the latter being a metal can filled with around fifty, one-inch diameter bullets: very unpleasant at the receiving end. With smooth bore and muzzle loading, it could fire two rounds a minute, a very efficient killer of soldiers. There were also rifled field guns of three-inch diameter bore, mainly ten-pounder Parrotts, used mostly for counter battery fire. The Confederates also had a few British made Whitworths with a range of over three miles. Their effect was more psychological as they were not very effective killers, not as accurate as the twelve-pounders or, of course, small arms' fire.

Small arms were mainly the muzzle-loading British made rifled muskets, or the Enfield or similar US Springfields, both highly regarded weapons. They fired a half-inch, soft lead bullet accurate at two hundred yards with a maximum range of five hundred yards, in competent hands achieving a rate of three shots a minute. Johnny said that conical-shaped bullets with an expanded skirt, invented by a French officer, Captain Minié, were widely used, giving increased range and accuracy, a great improvement.

Other improved rifles were being developed: the Henry repeater with twelve cartridges; new Springfield and Enfield rifles and muskets; several French models and, probably the best, Sharps and Merrill breech-loading rifles.

It was generally agreed, however, that weapons do not make a soldier necessarily better. They become killers for other reasons than just because they had a special kind of rifle. The muzzle-loading rifle or rifled musket remained the principle arm of the infantry.

After further talk of Johnny's own experiences and of his father, Colonel Juan, who was much experienced in the accoutrements of the US army at the time of the Indian Wars and, of course, his grandfather, Major John Collins of the 14th Hussars, killed during the Peninsular War, Johnny took his leave and promised to return with his full report for the general after two weeks.

Johnny returned to the Farm, was given the oak bedroom and a small office on the first floor with a view over the fields towards the north, an enchanting scene. He spent a few days visiting his few acquaintances at Oxford. The 11th Hussars were still in London and wined and dined him well. He also spent an evening with the 14th who were back from India. Doris's parents were very pleased to see him again and receive his news, as were his mother's family in the north.

He was the object of attention by various local ladies, especially the granddaughter of the old general in the village. The temptation was great but the forward, young lady was disappointed. Johnny felt it was best to behave.

So in due time he returned to the War Office.

At the War Office Johnny reported to the Staff Colonel who read through the report and said, 'Well done. We will go along now to see the general.'

The door plate read Major-General Charles Murray.

The general greeted Johnny warmly, saying, 'Well, Colonel Collins – don't look so surprised. I am having you promoted without purchase. It is well deserved – moreover it is perhaps more than coincidence that your grandfather was a great friend of and of immense help to my father, Charles Murray, in his undercover activities in the Peninsular War. I will read your report and then we shall talk about the contents.'

Johnny, of course, was delighted at the news and ever more so when upon leaving the general said that he was to report back to Lee after visiting his parents in Carolina and perhaps this time not to observe too closely the sharp end. The colonel he was told, would make the arrangements.

Johnny went off to his tailor to alter his uniform and order more for his future campaigning. Reporting back to the War Office, he received details of his passage back to America, leaving Liverpool in a week.

Back at the Farm, the Collinses were delighted with the advancement of Johnny to lieutenant-colonel and proposed to give a grand party to which the local gentry would be invited, especially the Cavalry general. Johnny said that he would be leaving from Liverpool in a week and proposed to visit both his regiment and his grandfather's, both of which were in London. He thought the party a grand idea and would also like to give one to the villagers and especially to meet those who were likely beneficiaries of his charity.

It was a glorious week for Johnny, very happy with his promotion and the obvious sincere friendship and good wishes from all.

At Liverpool he found his ship, somewhat old and relying on sails, with only auxiliary steam engines. The journey to Charleston would be slower than that from New York. At dinner the first night out his companion at table was a very charming, elegant French lady, who introduced herself as the wife of the French official in charge of France's affairs in the South. She remembered meeting the Collinses, Johnny's mother and father, at Columbia at various society gatherings.

'Well, we are almost old friends,' she said.

They enjoyed each other's company on the otherwise tedious voyage and all was calm until near the end of the journey when there was a somewhat unpleasant storm.

Both were good sailors but in the evening she said, 'Please take me to my cabin, I am not feeling too good.'

Well, of course, she invited him and, as she said, she was a little nervous.

Changing into something more comfortable she said, 'Please don't look,' a request which proved too much for Johnny and inevitably they retired to the bunk. The coupling was marvellous. She was very experienced and near the climax she speared his anus with a long middle finger, touching the prostate gland.

'My husband loves it,' she exclaimed as they exploded together. So ended Johnny's good intentions.

They landed together and left for Columbia where her husband stayed and they parted very good friends, promising to be careful when they met again, as obviously they would.

Part Six

America

1863–1864

25

So, Johnny came home to the plantation. Doris and the children were overwhelmed with emotion, the boy, James, was now nearly seven and growing a handsome one. Juan, now turned fifty years, and Johnny's mother were now running things, his grandparents having retired to Columbia to the family house there. All was well and flourishing and because of the slave system there was little manpower shortage due to the war.

Johnny said, 'I can only stay two weeks, I must go back to the war and catch up with the progress.'

In Johnny's absence a great battle had been won by Lee. Once more the Confederates were victorious, at Chancellorville near Friedricksburg in May of 1863, and now Lee was pressing north through Virginia, aiming eventually at New York, crossing the Mason-Dixon line into Pennsylvania. The Union Army was then commanded in the east by General Hooker, not very successfully, the army of the west by General Sherman and General Ulysses S. Grant, subsequently, in 1868, president of the United States, was in overall command.

Johnny reported to Lee whose headquarters were at Friedricksburg and the general said, 'Well, colonel, I see that you have been promoted, perhaps undeserved. Not very clever to get captured. You are, after all, an observer. You may go back to JEB, stay with him and do not wander off. Soon there will be an important battle and you should then spend some time with my infantry.'

The Confederate army was on the move to the north, cluttering the roads through the Blue Mountains from Friedricksburg through Culpeper, Winchester. The vanguard was already into Pennsylvania.

The Union army, with Hooker still in command, was poised to attack Lee's rear from Manassas but was warned by President Lincoln to be careful to protect Washington in case Lee changed direction. Hooker ordered the Union cavalry not just to reconnoitre around Culpeper, believing that Stuart's cavalry, thought to be some ten thousand strong but in reality more, would be severely mauled by his cavalry, comprising two divisions supported by two brigades of infantry.

Stuart was well aware of the Union movements and considered that they would choose the open ground around Brandy Station.

At dawn 9 June 1863, the crack of rifle fire out of the early morning mist from the Union position announced the opening of what was to be one of the greatest cavalry battles of all time. The advancing cavalry were at once attacked and balked by furious opposition from Stuart's Virginia Cavalry brigade.

As instructed by Lee, Johnny attached himself firmly to JEB's staff. The position was no sinecure, the general led from the front, as was customary, and with great dash, which example largely accounted for the success of his command. A year later he was mortally wounded at Yellow Tavern, too close to the sharp end and Stonewall Jackson was also gone, killed at Chancellorville.

Soon both cavalry forces were heavily engaged in a storm of charges and counter-charges by whole regiments, the infantry on each side closing in and taking part. Dust and smoke rose as a fog and in the consequent confusion could be heard bugles, shouts of orders, cries of pain, the clash of weapons and reports of revolvers and carbines. There was a real cavalry battle, raging throughout the day, the outcome long uncertain.

Later afternoon saw the end. Stuart had consolidated his position and the Confederate infantry were arriving in force, the Union cavalry general, Pleasonton's effort was spent and he withdrew from the field. It was a slender victory but even so Stuart had prevailed and, of course, ultimately that is what it is all about.

Lee was concerned about further attacks on the vulnerable strung out movement of his army, ever moving north. Hooker was moving his forces around but failed to gain the initiative. What became the Gettysburg campaign was under way.

Constant skirmishing by Pleasanton's cavalry was not very effective. Stuart's force was divided: two brigades to remain with the main body and the remainder with Stuart, moving with the other brigades to look and see behind the enemy towards Washington, a task he excelled at.

Hooker was replaced as commander by General Meade, a good soldier but untried in high command. He was, however, to prove successful.

Brandy Station was not to be compared with Balaclava: the former an unusual cavalry versus cavalry engagement, the latter a more usual charge against an objective, the guns.

Visiting Lee with Stuart after Brandy Station, Lee said to Johnny, 'I think it better to join my headquarters now that you have had your exciting stay with the cavalry. Ride occasionally with my aides. You will see much more.'

Now Johnny had faced an enemy more than most soldiers and was happy to get away from close quarter engagements.

The June summer weather was very hot the roads were full of dust and water was scarce. The marching soldiers were exhausted and many died from sunstroke. The victims of loss of sleep and heat exhaustion filled the ambulances. Stragglers were not deserters but sick men who were carefully rounded up by the cavalry rearguard. There was some relief from heavy thunderstorms which added to the misery by soaking clothes through.

Johnny noted the heavy burden carried by the infantrymen: gun, bayonet, cartridge and cap pouches, knapsack, canteen, mug, cooking pan, blanket roll, and rations. They were laden like beasts of burden.

Conditions were the same for both armies. Spurred on as they were by Lee and Meade to the inevitable junction where there would be a battle. It was absolutely necessary to cut off Lee's advance.

Pleasonton was ordered to seek another opportunity to attack the Confederates. It was considered that Brandy Station was not entirely a defeat, only a narrow victory for Stuart. It was not feasible to attack the advancing troops strung out on the inaccessible mountain roads. Pleasonton chose a place where the road emerged in a gap at Aldie, about a hundred miles south of Gettysburg, the probable location of the forthcoming battle.

Three brigades of Union Cavalry arrived near the gap at late afternoon where they found a confederate brigade encamping for the night. Surprisingly, the rebel infantry immediately attacked with spirit and the dismounted troopers were at a disadvantage, the rough country making manoeuvre difficult. Word was at once sent back to Lee who sent an aide to order the following troops to turn back. Johnny rode with the aide.

On arrival at the scene, they sought out the brigade commander who was at the front in the thick of the fighting. Johnny was taken aback by the hail of bullets, astonished that anyone could survive. He was heartened, however, by the apparent calmness of the infantrymen, who would certainly be alarmed by a cavalry charge situation where it was each to his own . . .

Back at headquarters, the aide reported that, in fact, all was going well and reinforcements were reaching the battle, holding the Union boys, the cavalry disadvantaged by the boulder-strewn ground.

Lee said to Johnny, 'Well, Colonel, how did you like your view at close quarters of infantry in action?'

Johnny replied that it was more frightening than the charge at Balaclava. There were so many things buzzing about like angry hornets that he would rather be mounted with a cavalry regiment. Lee retorted that infantrymen felt the same about the mounted men.

Meanwhile, Stuart had attacked from the rear and Pleasonton had to turn back part of his force to deal with the threat. Stuart's three brigades were finally driven into the gap with the other Confederates and Pleasonton withdrew to Aldie, claiming a complete victory. It was a disastrous day for the rebel cavalry.

In fact, losses to the Confederates were slight and, after all, victory's success must be measured by guns captured, casualties and prisoners taken. The effect on Lee was to guard more carefully against threats to the flanks of his advance. Several further attacks did occur, handled effectively by the Confederates.

On the Union side, Meade was settling in, appointed since President Lincoln had agreed that there was no other general with the army of the Potomac, the eastern force, and it was impracticable to detach a general from the army of the west. Towards the end of June, Union corps of infantry and cavalry were steadily moving north to cut off Lee's advance, inexorably armed at Gettysburg. Lee had now turned east out of the mountains. Neither side was fully aware of the other's positions, a lack of information which was to have serious consequences for Lee.

JEB Stuart was having a great time, rampaging and marauding behind the army of the Potomac right to the outskirts of Washington. He was confident that attacking the rear supply lines and communications of the enemy was more effective than joining Lee. This was a serious mistake. Lee was without his cavalry and totally lacking knowledge of Meade's dispositions.

If Lee had received information regarding the probable advantages of position the Union forces would have, he might well have chosen to avoid battle and press on northwards, fending off sporadic attacks by Meade's cavalry. As it was, a major encounter became inevitable at Gettysburg when initially Meade was surprised and on the first day the advantage lay with Lee.

130

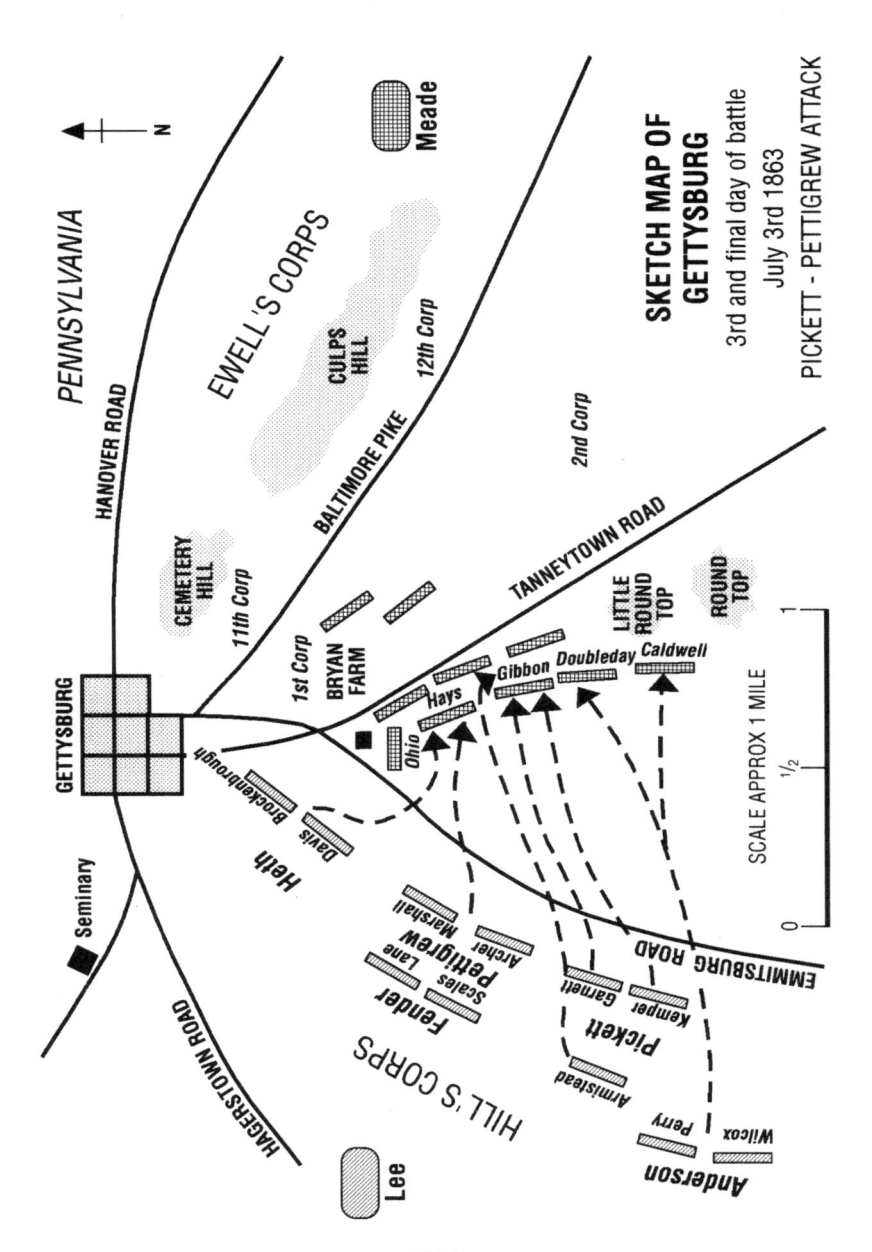

26

On the morning of 1 July 1863 the armies were advancing along the many roads at distances of one or two miles, all converging on Gettysburg. An advanced unit of three brigades was on the road in front of and deployed around the Lutheran seminary. Two Confederate brigades attacked frontally and another crossed in from the rear, forcing the blue-coats to either be cut off or retreat, so they pulled back.

By the afternoon, Hill's Corps, comprising a dozen brigades, were entering Gettysburg, the Union forces pulling back under heavy fire to positions on Cemetery Hill.

Johnny went early the following morning with an aide from Lee to the seminary where from the rooftop could be seen the fantastic sight of the two armies in position. Meade was on the high ground, by now well-established from Cemetery Ridge south along Culp's Hill down to Little Round Top and Round Top. The Confederates' three corps were drawn up in the low ground to the east, not exactly an advantageous situation, and there was considerable artillery activity in progress.

From their observations, the aide and Johnny gave Lee his first conception of Meade's dispositions, a formidable situation. During the second morning, Lee mounted a fierce attack on Culp's Hill and the Cemetery, only partially successfully. The Union artillery was well placed to enfilade the field from the northern flank and as fighting eased off there was little change on the field. A move to the Round Tops by the Confederates was blocked by a very gallant action in which a Maine regiment, led by a Colonel Chamberlain, a former schoolmaster, under intense fire from Confederate artillery, dashed into the oncoming rebels and prevented the occupation of the actual Tops.

Lee spent the rest of the day pondering over the morrow when of necessity he must mount the great assault. The artillery was to provide a cannonade such as had never been seen before, aimed at demoralizing the opposition. The attacking force comprised of brigades of Generals Pickett's, Heth's, Pender's and Anderson's divisions: in all, some fourteen thousand men, considered by most of Lee's Corps commanders to be totally inadequate. The plan was to rapidly advance across the half mile separating the forces and to break through before the enemy firepower could be brought to bear. The morning would show.

Johnny had met Major General George E. Pickett, a very flamboyant officer who, in fact, had not before manoeuvred a division.

However, meeting him the night before the assault, Pickett said to Johnny, 'Ride with me, Colonel. You will see some real action.'

Early on the morning of 3 July the enemies, facing each other along the Emmitsburg Road, were quiet. Only occasionally a burst of musketry or roar of a ranging cannon broke the calm before the storm, the fight for Culp's Hill. The Union artillery began the engagement, pounding the Confederate lines from well-placed batteries and there was considerable shelling from both sides, not in fact very effective because the Confederates were short of ammunition.

All being ready for the assault, the artillery opened up in earnest towards the Union lines, all guns firing as fast as possible; the heaviest bombardment in the war. Pickett was ordered to begin the advance and quickly marched his division off across the Emmitsburg road, the artillery giving some support in front of the advancing columns. Now the Yankee gunners, ideally placed in front of Bryan's Farm, opened up remorselessly on the advancing troops, cutting great holes in their formations which, such was their discipline, were at once closed up. The Ohio regiment

placed ideally on a flank poured down musketry fire.
Pickett's regiment finally reached the Union lines in an inferno of fire. Hand-to-hand fighting was vicious. The Union defenders were resolute and Pickett was forced to pull back. Johnny kept close to the general and found himself suddenly isolated in a bunch of furiously battling infantry, obliged to draw his sword in self-defence. He was astounded to see the weapon plucked away by a bullet which also took a large part of his hand with it. Regaining his senses, he rode out of the mêlée and was surprised to see Pickett way in front of him, quite unscathed. Johnny recalled Balaclava and the Earl of Cardigan riding out first from the charge, doubt being cast later that Cardigan had reached the guns. Similar doubts were expressed regarding Pickett as none, it seemed, could verify that he had been up to the enemy.

Johnny made his way unassisted to the dressing station where the surgeon regretfully was obliged to remove what was left of his right hand, sending him back to the base hospital.

Although only a small part of his army had been committed, Lee knew that he could not win at Gettysburg so retreated. The errant JEB returned too late and mounted a cavalry action to the rear of Meade on the fateful day, which was unsuccessful. The reversal of the Confederate fortunes marked the end of their success against the Union. General Grant became active in the field and won a great victory against the rebels at Fort Donaldson. Later on, Shiloh was a draw and battles at Vicksburg and Chattanooga were Union victories.

Grant continued against Lee in the Wilderness campaign, forcing him back to Richmond. General William Tecumseh Sherman, commander of the Western army, went into Georgia, capturing Atlanta, the state capital, which he sacked and burnt to the ground, continuing the savage devastation of the state into Carolina. He justified his brutality on the grounds that in order to win it was necessary to break the spirit of the people. Five Forks saw the end and Lee surrendered to Grant in April 1865. President Lincoln was assassinated, marring the victory. The Union was restored and slavery abolished.

27

Johnny ended up in the military hospital at Richmond. His arm was extremely painful and the nerves and tendons would take a considerable time to heal and to restore even partial use. In many ways his injury was worse than his father's loss of his arm. Whilst at the hospital he received orders to return to the War Office as soon as he was well enough. On being declared fit to travel, he went to the plantation where he was able to overcome the anxiety Doris, the children and his parents felt.

He said that he was ordered back to England. Doris was pregnant and it was decided that she should only come to England after the birth when she and the children were able to travel. Johnny's son, James, was quite disturbed by having his grandfather and father maimed in war and declared that he would never be a soldier. He would like to learn engineering and build railways.

Whilst at the plantation, Johnny went alone to Columbia to see his grandparents but secretly to contact his shipboard lover, the very experienced French lady, to sample more of her expertise in lovemaking. His trip was very successful. He felt much better and declared himself ready to leave for England. It was discussed that he would find a house in the village, seeks schools for the children and put James's name forward for Oxford in a few years' time.

Johnny left from Charleston on the fastest ship available. On the voyage, the inevitable shipboard romances were in evidence which Johnny avoided. The hanky-panky at Richmond was too close to think of sex with other women.

Liverpool was reached without delay from bad weather and Johnny took a train to London, firstly to go to the Farm.

Part Seven

England and France

1865–1871

28

At the farm the Collins family were distressed at Johnny's mutilation, another victim of war. He said that he would probably soldier on if required. Doris would come to England when the child was born and, depending on his visit to the War Office, they would settle in the village as he wanted James to go to Oxford.

At the War Office Johnny saw General Murray who said that he was sorry about the loss of his hand. If he wished to serve on, the general had a posting in mind for him. Meanwhile, he was required to update his previous report. In view of his incapacity he could stay at the office for a day or so and dictate to a clerk of the department. After taking some leave, the General would be in a position to discuss the future but it would be in order for him to bring his family to England.

So it was settled that he would remain in England and William Collins agreed with the suggestion that he seek a suitable house in the Village. William said that he knew of a house sufficiently large with a walled garden, stables and direct access on to the Heath, which was going cheaply as the owners were going abroad on short notice.

Indeed, the house was very adequate and Johnny completed the purchase without delay and moved in to get all in order for the family. Servants were no problem and he also acquired a smart trap and horse which would eventually be for Doris and the children.

He then took a well-earned rest, visited the regiment and Oxford to register James. Otherwise, he spent his time on the Farm, learning to ride without the use of his hand, his arm was fitted with a gloved hand, more as an ornament as it was immobile as far as the fingers went. His left hand was not very effective as he was not in the least ambidextrous.

Becoming bored, he went off to the War Office to find out about his new employment.

General Murray, pleased to see him back and ready to go, said that he had a splendid posting for him for which he was very well suited. Firstly, he would brief him on the situation on the Continent from where could be detected the rattling of sabres, particularly by Germany and France.

He said, 'The chief instigator is Prince Von Bismarck, the prime minister of Prussia, who is determined to establish Prussian domination in Germany and to undermine Austrian influence. The Austro-Prussian War has just ended with defeat of the Austrians and Kaiser Wilhelm I was now head of the North German Confederation. Bismarck intends to unite all the German states into one country and is creating a powerful modern army. France is also building up its forces and both are developing new weapons.'

He told Johnny that he was to establish a military mission in Paris, at the British Embassy, but accountable to the War Office. He would be provided with two experienced officers and ample funds. The German side would be taken care of by others. Apart from methods of training and deployment, the War Office were interested in infantry weapons and artillery. It was known that the Germans were developing small arms weapons.

France had adopted the American Gatling machine-gun which was just in use at the end of the Civil War and also the Browning. Johnny said that he knew about the Gatling which had several barrels and was operated by hand, rotating the breech, ever subject to stoppages. The Browning had not, he believed, been used in action. It was operated by the gas escaping after the cartridge was fired and also said to be unreliable. The general said that the French were also developing their own machine-gun, the Mitrailleuse, a multi-barrelled gun, breech-loaded, discharging small missiles in rapid succession. So far the British had no machine-gun.

As far as was known about artillery the General said, 'The French have a fine new twelve-pounder field gun and are known to be working on a revolutionary seventy-five millimetre piece and this we are most interested in. Fortresses are also being built or modernized along the eastern frontier. You may be able to take a look at these. You will be probably be in France for several years but are free to come and go to visit your family, whom I hope settle down in Hampstead.'

Johnny went to Paris to spy out the land and arrange facilities for himself and his two aides, finding suitable apartment accommodation not far from the embassy. The ambassador was very kind and helpful.

He said, 'I do not want to know what you are up to but you can always rely on me for assistance.'

He was quite fascinated by Johnny's story, which by any standards was remarkable. He knew the ambassador in Washington and said that he was a very useful envoy and was sure that he had done well by Johnny. The ambassador was also a graduate of Oxford so they had much in common.

29

In the winter of 1870 Johnny was in England for Christmas and the New Year and to arrange for James to enter Oxford. Doris was very happy with her family at the nearby farm and had many friends. William Collins and his wife, Alice, were celebrating the birth of their seventh child, a girl they christened Alice Louise. William was fifty-four years and Alice was in her mid-forties. It was a last fling and the baby made much of by their other children.

Johnny had come to England frequently during the intervening years to rest at home and report to General Murray who was well-pleased with his explorations. Visits had been made to the frontier and they were able to look over the fortifications at important locations, Verdun, Sedan, Maubeuge and others, particularly noting the garrisons and armaments.

James was installed at Oxford to study science, with a bent to civil engineering. He was a quiet, reserved, studious young man determined to do well and eventually achieve his aim, to build railroads. His tutor was very helpful and sometimes invited James to his house where the youngish wife made him very welcome in a seemingly motherly fashion.

One day she said quietly to the young man, 'Why don't you come on Sunday. It is very lonely as my husband goes away all day to see his parents.' James turned up expecting tea and conversation but the young woman had other ideas. James was a very attractive youth and his innocence made him even more desirable. On a pretext to reach for something behind him, she stumbled and literally fell into his arms. Pretending embarrassment, she struggled to get to her feet and quite accidentally, or perhaps not entirely, her hand pressed on his leg in a very private place. He was quite startled but did not resist when she, instead of removing her hand, explored further while at the same time kissing him very firmly. She undid his buttons and exposed a very fine, growing implement, drawing him up literally by tugging on it and leading him to the bedroom. They had a very thrilling time on the bed. What he lacked in experience, she made up for. He was very well-equipped and she loved his savage sexuality which she had unleashed. Such was their ardour that they had several climaxes lasting non-stop for the whole afternoon.

She said, 'James, I love you. You do it much better than my husband. We must be careful not to be discovered and we can have a marvellous time.'

The experience was good for James who opened out and continued his studies with increased interest.

The clouds were gathering over Europe and Johnny was kept very busy through the spring of 1870 and by summer the storm seemed about to break.

In July 1870 Bismarck by threatening attitude, goaded France to declare war on Prussia which was joined by other German States. Summer is a good time to start a war. The weather is likely to be favourable and it interrupts the enemies harvest. General Von Moltke attacked immediately at Sedan. Johnny was at the fortress by a fortunate chance and from a vantage point observed the hordes of infantry clad in the new field-grey uniforms, less conspicuous than the old brilliant scarlets and yellows, pour like a flood over the plain, unstoppable by the gunfire from the defences. The mass engulfed Sedan and swept on and the French emperor, Napoleon III, was captured. Johnny escaped by a route to the south and arrived back in Paris, quite shattered by what he had witnessed of the might of the new German army.

The French resisted ineffectually until a defeat at Mertz

caused the surrender of the army. It was all over in a few months. Paris resisted and was under siege until January 1871 when conditions had become impossible in the city. Johnny had remained until after the siege was lifted. The military mission was maintained for a few years afterwards.

A treaty was signed at Versailles, a location to prove favourable in future years for the conclusion of other wars.

The chief outcomes of the war were the creation of the German empire under Kaiser Wilhelm I with Bismarck as chancellor, to be called in later years 'the Iron Chancellor'.

A new departure in warfare was the use of air balloons, first invented by a Frenchman, Montgolfier. They were employed at the siege of Paris in observation and communications, to get messages out. Johnny managed to be allowed to make an ascent, a very startling experience at first and then remarkably enjoyable.

James continued his studies at Oxford and also his successful love life with the same lady and came down with a good degree and the same determination to go into rail. His father had now resigned from the army and was living in the village enjoying the good life.

Discussing James's future, Johnny said, 'I can probably get you attached to the Royal Engineers railway section for a year as a civilian where you will undoubtedly get first-class practical experience.'

This was arranged by Johnny pulling the strings at the War Office. Johnny considered that when James was ready, they would go back to America. His father, Juan, was now turned sixty years and would appreciate some help with the plantation. The following summer, after a round of farewells and letting the house to an officer stationed in the War Office, they all took ship from Liverpool, a fast steamer to New York.

Part Eight
America, Canada and Cuba
1872–1917

30

They were given a great welcome at the plantation; Johnny to relating his latest military adventures and expressing his intention to stay on with his father. James, whom his grandparents thought was a splendid young man, and John, a growing boy, who realizing James's intentions to have a life with the railroads, would most certainly follow on to take over when his father retired. It all worked out well. James went to New York and after asking around found out that his best opportunity lay in Canada.

Before the American Civil War all the railways used British know-how and equipment. The Civil War had emphasized the importance of the railways which up to then were confined to the east coast of the States. America then operated independently and a great expansion took place. By 1869 the Union Pacific had crossed the continent to the west coast, a formidable task. The Canadian Pacific Railroad was considerably later and was still under construction through the Rocky Mountains to Vancouver, the most difficult part.

James travelled to Toronto to seek employment with the company. He was interviewed by the chief engineer after seeing minor officials and writing a formal application. The chief quizzed him thoroughly about family background, education (Oxford!), practical experience (British Army!) and finally said, 'You may be just the man we are looking for.' He was offered a job as an engineer surveyor at railhead and beyond. It was likely that the chief surveyor would need to retire in a few years and James should bear that in mind. 'Kit yourself out at the company store,' he continued, 'and be ready to leave in a week. The base is at Edmonton and railhead camp beyond Jasper and into the Rockies. Our goal is Kamloops – Vancouver with a branch from Kamloops down to Calgary. As you will find out, the mountains are very spectacular but driving a railroad through them is a mammoth task. Good luck and bear in mind the possibilities of advancement in the future.'

James arrived at the camp beyond Jasper, literally where the rails stopped, and found the chief surveyor a rugged, somewhat elderly American who had been on the Union Pacific Railway some years earlier, very experienced and, as James found out, running on whiskey, which seemed not to impair his performance.

The chief said, 'Well boy, I see that I am to give you the full works. In a couple of days we will go up the line to the forward operation where you will be spending some months. Get kitted out at the store and you had better have a rifle and a revolver. There's no real danger but there are bear and wolves and good hunting for the pot. We are now away from the foothills and into the mountains proper.'

The Canadian Rockies are part of a mountain range, mainly of granite, running from Alaska through Canada to the south-west corner of America. To the west is the coastal basin and to the east the great plains. The crests of the Rockies, rising to over fourteen thousand feet, are the source of great river systems: the Yukon, the Missouri, etc. Gold, silver, copper, lead and coal are found. The coming of the railway opened up these resources. The railway knew where it was going but getting there was like steering a ship through innumerable rocky seas.

The party of some fifty strong set out on horseback, most as reliefs for surveyors and chainmen, the surveyors' assistants and labourers, who had been out, in some cases, for several months and with supplies on pack horses. A few miles ahead they reached the track-laying operations where gangs of Irish and Chinese labourers, mainly Chinese, of whom many remained behind, settling principally on the west coasts of America and Canada, laying and spiking rails on sleepers set to line and level by the surveyors working with them. The operation moved swiftly, each part depending on progress on the one ahead. All were well paid and working hard for production bonus pay.

For some miles further on the bed was prepared, laid and compacted to level, mostly so far straight. There were a few curves which were noticeably inclined in super elevation to accommodate the speed of the train. Ahead, the bed was being prepared, broken stone laid to line and level in layers, compacted by horse-drawn rollers. From there on surveyors were picking up the survey markers left behind by the forward surveyors and establishing the final track positions and markers for the laying of the road bed.

Further on, gangs were clearing trees, bushes and debris from the track line, levelling by cutting and felling; in most areas only minor adjustments. Elsewhere, blasting was necessary to carve a way out of the mountainside, sometimes a long and dangerous procedure inevitably accompanied by accidents, some fatal. At one location it was necessary to tunnel as the vertical cliff face precluded cutting a shelf.

Tunnelling was very skilled work and slow. Firstly, the surveyor had to establish the exit point and its relationship to the entry in direction and level so that the tunnel would arrive in the right place and height. This involved running a traverse above, often accessible with difficulty and requiring many trigonometrical calculations. Blasting was carried out by experienced miners. There was little risk of rock falls in the granite formation.

Recently, an error had occurred on a difficult tunnel which was curved on plan and with a considerable upgrade in level. When the two ends met, the forward part was five inches higher. The surveyor was shattered. The cost and loss of time in bringing the track down to the design level was horrifying and in his desperation the poor man committed suicide. In fact, the error was accommodated by re-designing the vertical curve over a reasonably short distance. Tunnelling requires a strong nerve in more ways than one. The tunnels were lined with timber or concrete.

Where the line passed close to the rock face of the mountain, avalanches of rock and snow were a considerable danger and shelters, roofing over the track, were built of timber and sometimes the rock face was covered with steel wire netting. Blasting, using very black gunpowder, was carried out by experienced miners so there was little risk of rock falls in the granite formation.

Whatever direction the track took, great emphasis was placed in maintaining gradients within the capacity of the rolling stock but sometimes, of necessity, envisaging the need for two locomotives and even a pusher as there was no other way to go.

From there on the track was marked by cairns through rough, uncleared country and requiring the party to diverge where cutting ledges or tunnelling was necessary. There were quite a few small bridges, culverts and embankments across long shallow valleys, minor suspension bridges over chasms. The valleys ran naturally from east to west. James thought that major bridge works would be just right for him.

The party, now fewer, reached the forward group, which had a most vital part in the whole venture, where wrong moves would be very costly and perhaps lead to rerouting of the track, a situation requiring considerable skill and nerve by the man on the spot. The chief was in a hurry as the whiskey was getting low, so without much ado passed James over to the leading surveyors.

Maps they had were very good, made by excellent cartographers over many years and the route of the railroad had been carefully drawn up on the information available. On the ground, the actual location was beset by many considerations and problems arising in order to choose the most workable way. The leading surveyor was very skilled and experienced, as needs be. There was always clearing of trees, obstacles, etc. in order to set out the line on the ground marked at regular intervals by iron pegs set to levels and marked by whitewashed stone cairns. In fact, it was a slow process, particularly when arriving at places where tunnels were required.

It was a rugged existence. James was quite content and learned much. He stayed out for longer periods than usual, even up to a year. The old chief surveyor visited periodically and more or less approved their performance. They respected his enormous knowledge and experience, welcoming his helpful advice and suggestions, which were invariably correct.

In the course of time, James passed back to work with the other major survey teams and made more frequent visits to the railhead base camp where he met the chief engineer and in conversation expressed his ambition to join the engineering department.

The chief said, 'Well, we shall think about it.'

The inevitable happened to prevent James's move. The old chief surveyor dropped dead, overcome by the whiskey at last, and James was appointed in his place, a big step on the way. He was very pleased and determined to carry on the old man's good work. At a convenient time, he took a short leave and went by the now very efficient railway network to South Carolina to visit his parents. Johnny, his father, had now taken over the plantation, his grandparents having retired. Brother John was finishing at Harvard and would work with his father, so James was free to follow his life on the railroad.

In 1885 the line to Vancouver was complete and work was progressing on the difficult section across the Rockies to Calgary. James by now had achieved his ambition to join the engineering department and was appointed to take charge of the major bridge. His performance was very satisfactory and he gained a good reputation with Canadian Pacific. As the years passed, he felt like a change. The railway system over the major routes was more or less complete and it was time to move on.

Through the grapevine, James learned that the New York based Erie Railroad company were expanding their network and were planning to construct a line to the great lakes, to be known as the Grand Trunk Erie Railroad, and were looking for a chief engineer. It was 1893 and construction was scheduled for the following year.

James took a leave due to him and went to New York where he had a successful interview with Erie and terminated his job with Canadian Pacific. Initial survey and planning, compared with the problems in the Rockies, was easy, as was the advantage of working out from New York. Very soon the track was open some miles into New York State with few problems and Buffalo lay ahead, the whole distance around six hundred miles of track.

Whilst spending most of his days out on the job, James was able to reach New York easily and decided to take an apartment there. He found a suitable place in fashionable Manhattan which he purchased outright. His years away in the wilds on considerable salaries had made him reasonably wealthy. Also, his life had been so far without women, not by inclination, so he was able to find the occasional girl. There were always some willing ones to spend a night with him, nothing permanent.

The site was frequently inspected by the vice-president who was responsible for the new line. Using a specially fitted coach with proper living accommodation, a widower, he travelled with his daughter. She was no longer young, approaching thirty years, somewhat plain-looking but with a good figure; that is, bedworthy. She was very reserved and very likely still a virgin, Daddy's little girl. James was forty years old and had already considered that if he were to marry it would have to be soon. Cora, he thought, would be a good match, not unattractive, and there was the father with considerable influence in the railway world.

James was often invited to dine at the coach and insinuated himself very carefully into Cora's life. He was very assiduous in his attentions and very often touching her quite intimately, by accident, as it were. One fine evening, her father retired early with a headache and James took Cora for a walk in the pleasant summer countryside. He was thinking,

'This is the time'. They sat resting on a grassy bank. He quite gently kissed her. She was very shy and rigid from a newly felt emotion; something she had never before experienced, the hardness of a man's body. Very gently, James caressed her quite well-developed breast, kissed enthusiastically and snuggled up. Soon they were lying down and very carefully he explored under her skirts until he reached the great divide which he found, to his surprise, to be warm, wet and sticky, but very definitely closed up. Now was not the time for deflowering, nor the place, so he just worked away gently with his fingers, feeling her clitoris harden until she gave a sudden shiver and a small cry. Enough until next time. They became very fond of each other and for certain father was aware that something was afoot but was not opposed to an up-and-coming young man courting his daughter.

James proposed marriage which delighted Cora and together they went to Daddy, who gave his consent with a chuckle saying, 'It's about time.'

The wedding was a quite splendid affair. The newly-weds departed on the Chicago express and consummated the marriage in a rattling, swaying bunk, very successfully. Cora was absolutely blissful, her sexual desires freed and totally in love with James. They went on from Chicago to Niagara Falls, staying at hotels at the American and Canadian Falls, wonderful places for a honeymoon.

They bought a house at Yonkers, not too far from New York. With uncanny foresight, James kept the Manhattan apartment a secret. Cora was not particularly exciting and there might be others.

When the railroad was completed, James was put in charge of the company workshops and also the maintenance and repair of the permanent way, bridges, and signal system; a very responsible, well-paid position. Cora was pregnant and in due course gave birth to a son who was christened James, after his father.

When baby James was old enough, they took a trip to England and visited the Farm. The Collins family were delighted. All was well with them. The two eldest sons had gone off to the colonies, one to Australia and the other New Zealand. One daughter was married and living in the village.

31

No sooner back from England, James was off to Cuba on loan to the government to report on the very important railways which transported the sugar cane and which had been damaged in the recent upheaval. James had been sought out because of his experience, backed by a group of companies heavily involved in Cuban sugar, among them the president of Erie. He would probably be away for six months.

In 1895, a revolution had broken out in Cuba, the native Cubans fighting for liberation from the Spanish who had been there for some three hundred years. The revolution caused heavy losses to American investments and the US government was obliged to intervene militarily. The sinking of the US battleship *Maine* was the final straw and naval engagements quickly defeated the Spanish fleet. Troops were landed, the fighting was soon over and a treaty was signed in 1898. The US governed until independence in 1902.

James's brief was to inspect the railways which carried the sugar cane on great open, basket-like wagons and also the cane crushing plants, to initiate repairs and to order new equipment as required. A passage was arranged with the US navy to Santiago de Cuba which was firmly in American hands, as by now was most of Cuba. At nearby Palma Soriano he would find a major centre for sugar collection and crushing run by a Cuban manager who was instructed to afford him any assistance.

The Cuban was, indeed, a very able fellow, providing James with guides, horses and a suitable wagon-cum-carriage for baggage and supplies. He told James that he did have a problem. Staying with his family was a Spanish lady, widowed by the death of her husband at the hands of the revolutionaries. Probably James would be able to help. The Spanish were not welcome in Cuba. James met the lady, Señora Arabella, at the house and was at once smitten by her. She was in her mid-thirties, slim but of good figure, not beautiful but strikingly handsome. He explained to her that he would be more than willing to help her but that he would be travelling most of the time.

She said, 'Take me with you. I can take care of your living arrangements and I will be much safer with you.'

Inevitably, from the beginning they made love, both enamoured with each other and very passionate. In a flash James knew why he had kept his pied-à-terre in New York a secret. It was made for Arabella, their love nest.

The work went very well. James organized repairs, improvements and suggestions for extensions to track and plant. Arabella turned out to be a very talented artist and was able to illustrate his reports with splendid drawings and water colour paintings.

As the work drew to a close, James must return to America. He said that he could obtain the necessary papers for her to travel with him if she wished. There was no doubt that she would. She vowed that she would stay with him forever, even though he could not marry her. They took passage to New York and he settled Arabella into the apartment and together they found other Spaniards who had been in Cuba with whom she could associate and make friends.

James reported to the Erie president, who was very pleased with the good work he had carried out in Cuba. The sugar industry was recovering from the troubles and the US investors well-satisfied.

He told James, 'You deserve a step up the ladder. I need a new vice-president in charge of operations and I am sure that you will fit the bill.'

They settled down to the good life. America was prosperous. James was kept very satisfied by Arabella and he scarcely looked at other women. It was a great boon not always to be conscious of sex. However, he did manage enough steam to make a daughter from Cora, whom they named Cora-Ann.

James became involved with Cornell University in New York State, where engineering had its own particular college and early in the twentieth century was on the board of governors. In due course, his son, James, would be enrolled at Cornell.

In 1914, war broke out in Europe with England and France with other allies against Germany, Austria and the Turkish Ottomans. The US maintained neutrality but the sinking of the *Lusitania* imperilled that attitude and America began arming. The *Lusitania*, a British passenger liner, was sunk without warning by a German submarine in May 1915. One thousand lives were lost and more than one hundred were prominent Americans, causing the US to prepare for war.

In 1916, Germany began unrestricted submarine war during which, inevitably, American ships were involved and lives lost. In April 1917 American declared war on Germany. An American Expeditionary Force was assembled under General Pershing and sent to France, becoming involved in the fighting early in 1918. Almost certainly, the American intervention ended in the defeat of Germany.

Part Nine

England and France

1917–1918

32

At the beginning of 1918, Europe was close to collapse. More than three years of a terrible war in which millions of soldiers had been killed or maimed had ravaged the land and caused misery to many innocent civilians and bereaved families. The belief that their cause was just and that God was on the side of both adversaries was wearing thin. The war was no longer a great crusade. The bitter and costly trench warfare, with enormous losses, was measured in yards of ground won or lost. Belgium and France suffered most. The savagery also raged in Italy, the Balkans, Mesopotamia, now divided into Iraq and Iran, and Palestine.

The entry of America brought the only hope of an Allied victory and indeed was to be the deciding factor of the war. Some hundred thousand American troops were already in France, not yet committed to battle but continuing their training. Soon it was planned that more than one million men would be on the way. 'The Yanks are coming' was chanted with some derision, even in a song called 'Over There', but afterwards it was acknowledged that in 1918 the Americans won the war.

An attack to finish the war was made by the British in the summer of 1917 at Ypres. An unparalleled artillery barrage was followed by a hundred thousand men going 'over the top'; that is, scrambling out of the trench into a hail of bullets and shrapnel, with the odds against survival. A quarter of a million men were lost for a few miles gained and a resumed stalemate.

In England, the population suffered shortages of food and clothing caused by German submarine action and the demoralizing effect of bombing by Zeppelin airships and bomber aeroplanes. Food queues and profiteering became part of the national scene. The British were frayed of temper and there was great dissatisfaction but the people could still joke with a *Punch*-style humour.

In March 1918, the Germans began a great offensive which was to repeat the advance of 1914 and take them once more to the outskirts of Paris. The opening fury of the German bombardment was paralysing, a new type of mustard gas shell mixed with high explosive missiles of all calibres. British return fire was quelled by relentless counter-battery action: a perfect hell. As the artillery fire lessened in No Man's Land, waves of grey clad men swept out of the trenches, encouraged by rage against the foe and alcohol. The Germans issued spirits before an attack, the British after. In a month they had advanced an incredible fifty miles. The Germans kept up a series of offensives until August, when the tide irrevocably turned.

The Americans were in action towards the end of the first offensive and, much against Pershing's opposition, they were amalgamated into the Allied Command. Pershing did succeed in the Americans having their own command. He also initiated the principle of having a supreme Allied Commander and approved the proposal that the French General Foch was responsible for the strategic direction of the war.

33

James was at Cornell University studying engineering when America declared war on Germany. With his father's approval, he interrupted his studies and offered his services to the Marines. He was accepted for an officer's short training course and passed out as a second lieutenant. He was posted to the Marines in the 2nd Division. The division left for France and was based in a rear area for training prior to going up the line. It was early spring and the countryside very pleasant, with good estaminets and restaurants with food and wines to their liking.

One particular estaminet, which also functioned as a brothel, was patronized by James's company officers. Cornell was a coeducation establishment and James was no virgin and was happy to find sexual relaxation at their virtual 'club'.

When James and three other platoon officers first went to the estaminet, having a bottle and looking around at the girls, they spotted one immediately. She was not very beautiful but with a jolly disposition, acting as though she enjoyed her work. Almost simultaneously the four said, 'I am going to have her.'

So they cut cards and James was the last in line. The girl trooped up the stairs with number one who soon came down and told the next in line that she would be at the door of her room. James's turn came and he was not slow to mount the stairs where she was waiting. The room was tidy with a very large bed and in one corner an enamel bidet on a stand which she obviously had used. James removed his uniform jacket and trousers and got on with the job. Indeed, she was very nice and he experienced a very satisfying ejaculation.

She also was a little red in the face and he realized that she had also had an orgasm, unusual for a professional, but supposedly overcome by four successive young men.

She kissed James, exclaiming, 'We do not kiss our patrons but . . . *tu es vraiment tres gentile, cheri. Viens toi souvent, si tu veux.*'

So they all did and that was one problem solved.

Training went on for many weeks, inevitably sorting out the weakest, surprisingly, but it did sometimes occur, James was promoted to captain and given a company.

In May, the Germans mounted another all-out offensive, advancing to the river Marne, only thirty miles from Paris. When it appeared that all could be lost, the end for the Allies, General Pershing offered the 2nd Division, followed up by the 3rd. Lorries and buses were made available at once by the French and the Americans. Fresh, eager troops, wearied with endless training, arrived near Belleau, close to the Marne. The 2nd Division took over prepared trenches at Belleau Wood a place to be well-remembered, and the 3rd to the south across the river. This was where the breakthrough would probably happen.

The Americans were very well-equipped with weapons developed during the build up period from 1915-1917. The latest Springfield rifles and Hotchkiss machine-guns, even their clothing and boots, were the envy of other armies: American know-how at its best.

The trenches in front of Belleau Wood were not front line standard but unlike those in Flanders, were free from knee-deep mud. The Germans out in front were only a short distance across No Man's Land, measured in yards not miles. James's company set about improving the trench system, erecting more wire at night, when the first casualties occurred from random Maxim machine-gun fire. In the daytime, the occasional shell burst nearby with little effect. The slightest visible movement brought a well-aimed Mauser rifle bullet. For the present, the Germans were resting and preparing for what could prove to be the final push of the war and victory but they, like the British, were battle-weary, exhausted and unfit for serious combat.

Towards the end of May, it began at one o'clock of a still night soon shattered by a massive bombardment of guns and trench mortars at first using gas ammunition on all targets. The American 2nd Division received more than its share, being positioned as the stop end of where the breakthrough was anticipated. Hundreds of high explosive shells followed the gas. The night became a sheet of flame, the earth shuddering under the avalanche of projectiles. In the trenches, the men were hampered by wearing hideous gas masks and could only crouch and get whatever cover they could, except for the few sentries who were obliged to look over the top. The few dugouts were crowded with jostling sweating soldiers. Entrances were covered with wet blankets against the gas. Occasionally, an unlucky shell fell and burst in the trench, killing those outside and in some bunkers causing collapses and burying men alive.

At first light, covered by the smoke, dust and gas clouds, the German grey-clad infantry were almost at the end of the trenches before they were sighted. The men scrambled out of the dugouts to find Germans already in the trench. In James's company's position, fierce hand-to-hand fighting cleared the trench. The Germans were no match for the fresh Americans, most of them rough and tough farmboys. The position held but by the afternoon the line was obliged to fall back to the prepared positions behind. The German advance was held and the Americans proved that they could fight.

The 2nd division had held the attack and stopped the German advance. It was now their turn to assault the enemy position inside Belleau Wood. Marines went over the top at dawn, leading the division. James's company in the forefront were immediately under heavy-machine-gun fire and some men went to ground for cover, a natural instinct. James urged them forward and at his inspiration they rushed on, bayonets ready to thrust at the grey uniforms as they reached

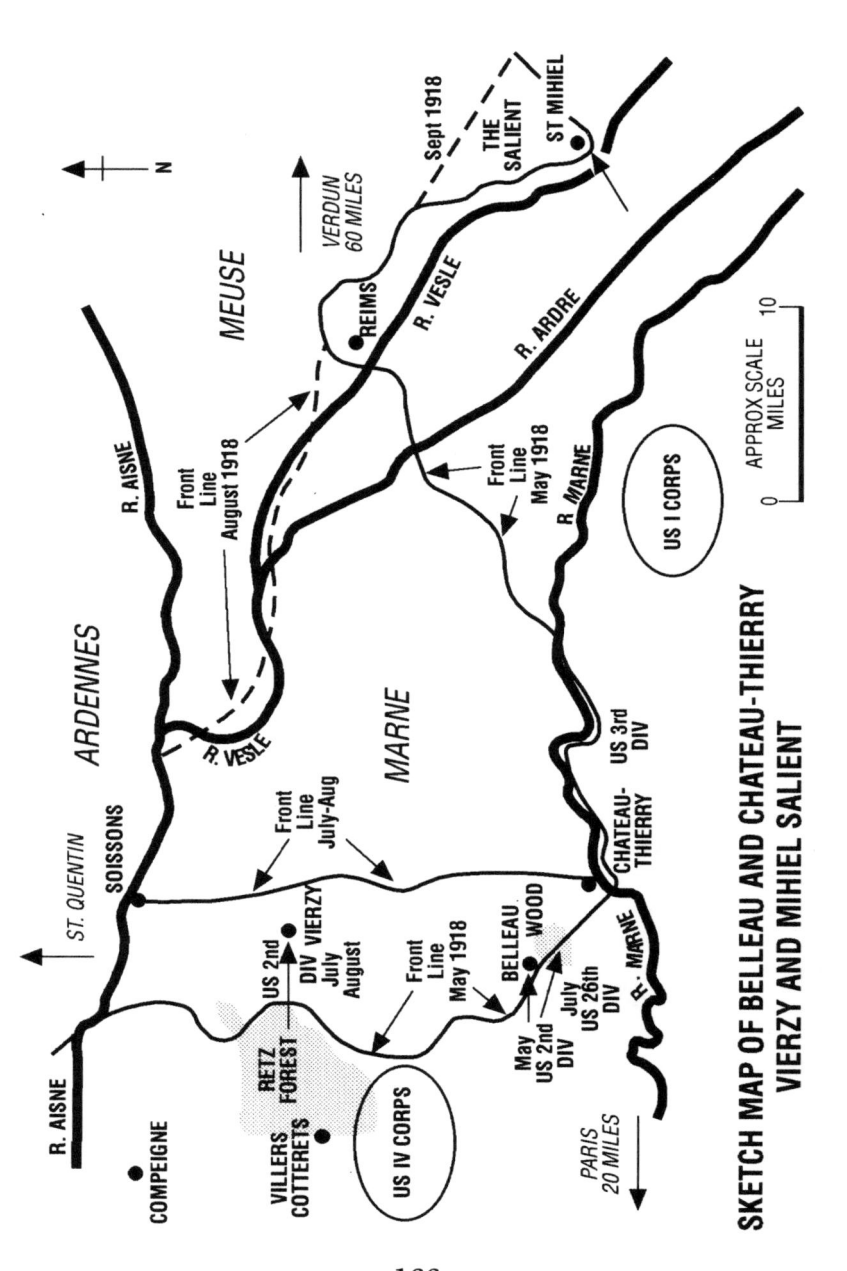

SKETCH MAP OF BELLEAU AND CHATEAU-THIERRY VIERZY AND MIHIEL SALIENT

the enemy trench. James was using a rifle, very effectively better than his revolver. The Boche were surrendering if they could and those retreating were followed by a hail of bullets. A machine-gun post towards the rear was overcome and the company reached the hill which was the battalion's objective and commenced digging in. Casualties had been surprisingly light, a few killed and wounded, and replacements were readily available from the massive influx of troops across the Atlantic on the great passenger liners; safe from U-boat attacks due to their superior speed.

At dusk the same evening, they moved forward again over open ground to gain another part of the wood. In the open fields, they were cut down by a murderous fire from both flanks and were forced to go to ground. Obviously, the enemy artillery would soon be raining shells on them in the open so they made a supreme effort and reached the comparative safety of the forest. James during the advance under the machine-gun fire felt something tug at his arm and shoulder, a burning sensation. Two bullets had just grazed his flesh. Many fell before they reached the trees but the division pressed on and gained and held a mile. It was not the greatest battle of the war but compared with previous gains of a few yards at heavy cost, a remarkable achievement. More importantly, Paris was saved as the German High Command decided to end the Marne offensive.

The division was relieved and pulled back to a reserve area to recover, reorganize and make up their losses. General Pershing praised them for their splendid showing at Belleau Wood and distributed medals for gallantry to those whose conduct had earned them.

They returned to the line at Villers Cotterets at the centre of the great bulge created by the German advance in May. It was early July. All was quiet in the sector, only occasional shelling and activity, or night raids to worry the enemy and the capture of prisoners to gain information. From his company, James formed a special raiding group of the more daring men who were also physically suited. He led several excursions into the Boche trench opposite. Stripped of all but essential weapons and with blackened faces they crawled over No Man's Land, invariably surprising the Huns. They were in and out before they were discovered, except on one occasion when the sentries were extra alert and the raiding party was forced to fight its way out, with the loss of some men.

Since the commitment of US troops to the front line in May, the build-up had been swift. Besides the 2nd division, there were now at the front two army corps comprising six divisions in all. There was later a joint Australian-American Corps which was highly successful. The mixed battle army of US and Australian forces worked well, both having similar push and vitality which culminated in defeat for the Boche.

In mid-July, the front in the area of Soissons, Villers-Cotterets erupted in a massive US artillery bombardment: a mighty thunder, added to by planes dropping bombs and machine-gunning the trenches and lines of communication. As the barrage lifted, the Americans, aided by tanks, surged forward. The Germans fell back in disarray and the 2nd US Division reached their objective, Vierzy, an advance of nearly ten miles. The storming of Vierzy was achieved against strong German reserves rushed in to halt the advance. Several attacks by the 2nd division were repelled, the battalion being riddled by machine-gun bullets. James's company was ordered to attack a nest of guns holding up the line across a ravine. The company advanced, using the scant cover available, and were forced to ground by the intense fire. James realized that only a sudden, all-out rush at the emplacements would succeed.

He passed the word down to the platoons, 'When you see a red Very signal flare, go all out'. Their casualties were high, half the company were wiped out, but the following troops were able to advance into Vierzy without more serious hold-ups.

Whilst the attack on the whole Soissons front was successful, the slaughter was awful. The advanced dressing stations were overwhelmed with the wounded. Germans and Americans lying side by side in farmyards, with blood over everything, some dying or already dead.

As night fell, the order came for a further attack in the morning. The troops tried to get some sleep. They were suffering from thirst, the canteens were empty and available sources dried up by the unusual demands.

James dozed fitfully on the ground that night thinking of what horror the morning might bring. That day had not been too awful, apart from the attack on the machine-guns, for which he was to be awarded a decoration, but tomorrow?

At dawn, the division moved forward. No surprise attack this second day and immediately they found themselves faced by a reinforced enemy who were, in fact, a division of the guards Corps, an elite unit. They were met by a solid hail of machine-gun bullets and the leading companies were wiped out. Tanks arrived, lumbering forward, impervious to the small arms' fire, followed by waves of infantry. Then shells from the German artillery fell among them. Some tanks were hit and burned up in flames. Men were falling all around. Somehow, sufficient men broke through, driving the Boche back. James's company, what was left of it, took an old trench and held on against a counter-attack. Others on both flanks were digging in furiously. Get down or die.

The rest of the day was awful and as night came on those who were alive tramped out under the light of German flares, back to the Forest of Retz, the place where they started from.

The 2nd division lost nearly five thousand men. James's battalion was decimated, the division fit only for rebuilding. They moved back to recover and make up their losses. James was promoted to major. Advancement was swift in the infantry. An infantry officer's chance of survival in an attack was largely a matter of luck. In spite of little difference in dress and appearances, the leader, be he officer or sergeant, was a target.

They were in the old camp and James visited and relieved

his emotions with the estaminet lady who said, '*Ooh la la.* A grand officer now and, my, how you have grown. It must be hungry.'

The general addressed the regiment, congratulated them and presented the awards for gallantry. He told them that they would be wanted soon and they would be equipped with whatever was improved or new.

James's company was augmented and he was given a captain to take charge of and organize his raiders, a concept which had proved worthwhile and was now instituted in other companies.

In September, the 2nd division were back at the front in the area between Verdun and Metz at and around St Mihiel, three US army corps comprising eight divisions and supported by three French divisions. The assault was to take out the rest of the bulge remaining from the German advance in other areas.

Foch stressed to Pershing how vital this operation was and Pershing said, 'We will do it, don't worry.'

Time was vital since strategic planning called for the same US forces to mount another operation in the Argonne section.

At dawn one day in mid-September, the Allied artillery let off a tremendous barrage directly at the enemy positions in front of St Mihiel and to the rear lines. The 2nd division Marines took off and, in spite of the shelling, the Boche opened up with withering fire. Pressing on regardless, they overran the trench in front, the barrage already lifted and concentrating on the rear. Waves of the assault were moving along the whole front: irresistible, the enemy retreating or being taken prisoner. A considerable force of US and French tanks also advanced with and behind the foot soldiers. By midday the Allies had advanced ten miles into the centre of The Salient and only halted progress as night came. They were elated and ready, unperturbed, for the next day's fight.

The following day it was over. The Salient was cleared and

the enemy line straightened out, removing a thorn that had been a great nuisance for too long. The 2nd division had been held up at a strongly fortified village. James was ordered to go in and force an entry for the rest of the battalion. He selected a squad of Marines and led the way, coming under intense fire. James, up with them, was hit in the thigh by a bullet, felling him to the ground. He was soon reached by the stretcher-bearers and carried away to the advanced dressing station which, for a change, was not busy, casualties being light.

James arrived at a base hospital by ambulance train. His wound was not serious, no bones broken, but the exit of the bullet had removed quite a lot of flesh. However, a couple of weeks would see him walking with the aid of a stick.

James's parents had received the usual wire saying that he had been wounded in action but were relieved to see his photograph in the New York papers with other wounded at The Salient. Sitting up in a hospital bed, he looked remarkably well.

In August, the British mounted a great attack on a wide front to the north of the lines towards the ultimate goal, the fortress-like Hindenburg line. It was partly successful and the Germans were disheartened by their defeat. The British and Colonial troops had engaged fifty-seven German divisions, with all they could throw at them: guns, tanks, planes, gas, shells and bombs and six of the best divisions in the initial attack. Some fifty miles of enemy held land was taken, but at a cost of one hundred and eighty thousand casualties.

The Americans were to continue the assault on the Hindenburg line to the area south of the British. The move of the US army in a short time was a masterpiece of organization and all was ready on the last day of September.

James more or less discharged himself from the hospital and made his own way back to the battalion, mended but with a limp and a walking cane. The marine colonel told James that he had considered a new method of command.

He himself would remain at the rear where he could overlook the battalion advance, instead of the traditional leading from the front, also he would be in contact with division.

He said, 'James, the men will accuse me of cowardice but the advantages gained make it worthwhile. You will go with the companies and keep in touch by runner. I hope that your leg will not hinder you.'

The morning of the attack was shrouded in fog so dense that the runners had difficulty in keeping in touch with the next man. The Germans were equally frustrated and the battalion advanced with little resistance. By midday, the fog cleared and the Marines were all over the place and it was sometime before they became organized into a coherent force. The Hun now put up a strong fight but the attacking US divisions and the US-Australian Corps smashed on, crossing the impregnable Hindenburg line over a five mile stretch where the main obstacle, the St Quentin Canal, was tunnelled underground.

The 2nd division was through with few casualties. James had managed well and the colonel's tactic worked satisfactorily.

The next morning the dawn was heralded by a rain of gas and high-explosive shells. Bit between teeth, the Allies pressed on and by nightfall it was over. The famous line was broken and the Germans were in retreat. James was keeping up with the companies, by now very weary and in pain. The German artillery at the rear put down heavy barrages on the Allies to help their troops to fall back to new positions. James was hit by a large arrow-like piece of shrapnel which lodged in his shoulder: a serious wound, felling him unconscious.

Marshall Foch was in his glory. The German Allies were in disarray, the Turks and Bulgarians were finished, Austria was collapsing. Nevertheless, the German Supreme Command would not surrender until forced by the desperate military situation and the plight of the German civilians. Early November 1918 saw the end of a horrific war which tore Europe apart.

*

James ended up at a base hospital with the lump of shrapnel still embedded in his shoulder. The journey for him was extremely painful and most of the time he was barely conscious.

At the base the metal was removed by an operation lasting several hours. Bones had been smashed and flesh horribly torn. It was decided to send him to England where there were surgeons and hospitals vastly experienced with war wounds after four years of war. James was taken to the prestigious King Edward the Seventh Hospital for Officers in London, where hopefully his shoulder would be repaired. He would be in hospital for several weeks and then be placed in a special convalescent home for treatment.

In common with others, James was in *The Times*'s lists of officers returned wounded from the front. These lists were scanned every day by many readers. At North End Village, Elizabeth Jenkins, formerly Collins, William Collins's eldest daughter, now married to a West End jeweller, was running through the latest column.

'Major James Collins, US Marine Corps – King Edward VII Hospital. That must be the son of James Collins of New York,' she pointed out to her daughter Elsie. 'We must go to see him.'

Elizabeth was a strikingly handsome gentlewoman, a well-loved lady with several children and a successful marriage, living in the house at one time owned by James's grandfather, Johnny Collins.

They duly went to see James, finding him not very well but recovering.

'I am your Great Aunt Elizabeth, William Collins's daughter, and this is my daughter Elsie. As you may know, William Collins died in 1906 and the farm has gone.'

The visit was of necessity short as James was far from well but they promised to come often and would write to his father in New York.

In the spring of 1919, James, then at the convalescent home for officers, was able to visit the village and stay with

Aunt Elizabeth. Elsie was an attractive girl of unusual intelligence, about the same age as James and quite unattached. They went for walks over the heath and sometimes visited one of the well-known inns for a glass or more of wine. The inevitable happened. By coincidence, they sat one evening in a place very close to where John Collins had laid down with his sweetheart, over a hundred years earlier. They were sheltered from the wind and prying eyes, it being a favourite pastime of others to spy on lovers. They kissed as they had before, but not in a cousinly fashion, and James's hand wandered over her breasts and then down between her legs. She was vivaciously enthusiastic, inviting further action by spreading her legs. James removed her drawers with her ready help and unbuttoned himself. Although apparently a virgin, entry was easy, the membrane partly torn already. They both enjoyed the encounter then and several times afterwards and one day James proposed marriage which she gladly agreed to.

Elsie's family were delighted and her father said, 'You can choose the ring from my shop in Regent Street, where you will find the most beautiful selection in London.'

When James was fit to leave the convalescent home, his shoulder satisfactory although such wounds are never wholly better and pain would sometimes occur, he obtained his discharge from the military attaché at the American Embassy.

He and Elsie married, as had other members of the family at Hampstead parish church, James wearing his uniform for the last time. They honeymooned at fashionable Torquay in the West Country, a surprisingly warm place where even palm trees grew.

On their return they made reservation from Liverpool to New York, promising to return often for holidays which, in fact, they did the following year, with James's parents.

Part Ten

Epilogue

EPILOGUE

Back in America with his new bride, they were welcomed profusely by James's parents and stayed with them at the house outside New York. It was agreed that Elsie would stay there until he finished his studies at Cornell.

James settled down to a position on the Erie Railroad and also helped his father to start up and operate a taxi business in New York which was very successful. In time, James was very active and eventually became president of the railway, the taxi business flourished and he continued his father's activities on the university board. Occasionally, they went to South Carolina to the family plantation.

After the war, America was very prosperous, having benefited by developing industrial and manufacturing capacity to supply the Allies who were desperate for everything the US could provide. This relationship continued for many years as the war-impoverished countries were in a sorry position and unable to develop their own resources.

So James, his grandfather, and great-grandfather, were all victims of wars, injured in battle, and his great-great-grandfather, John Collins, was killed in action.

On the English side, when William Collins died in 1906, his three daughters were married and living in the village. His four sons had gone abroad. The Farm broke up, the house was taken over by the Architect who was developing the Hampstead Garden Suburb, a new conception in housing. The Farm land became the eighty acre playing fields.

During the early months of the Second World War, the Germans parachuted a very large landmine which exploded on top of some very tall trees, damaging most of the village houses at the roof-top and below, rendering them uninhabitable. The remaining Collinses left to live in Hampstead or further afield.

Cyprus 1995/96